CAPTAIN GRINGO GOES DOWN

As the slimy muck reached Gringo's knees he froze in place, looked down, and muttered, "Oboy, now you've done it."

He had blundered into quicksand and, even standing still, he was slowly sinking. Soon he was up to his thighs!

He tried moving toward the reeds at the edge of the bog. The scummy goo rose faster. By the time he gave up his crotch was buried, too. Gringo shuddered, but quickly got a grip on himself and growled aloud, "Easy now. You got into this alone and you have to get out of it alone. You're too far from camp for anyone to hear and... hey, how come I'm so stupid?"

He drew his .38 and fired three shots in the air. It was the recognized distress call.

The muck was up to his rib cage when he heard someone coming. "Over here! Watch your step! I'm stuck in quicksand!"

But then that someone starting shooting at him!

Novels by
Ramsay Thorne

Renegade #1

Published by
WARNER BOOKS

Renegade #21

RIVER
OF
REVENGE

Ramsay Thorne

WARNER BOOKS

A Warner Communications Company

WARNER BOOKS EDITION

**Copyright © 1983 by Lou Cameron
All rights reserved.**

Warner Books, Inc.,
666 Fifth Avenue,
New York, N.Y. 10103

 A Warner Communications Company

Printed in the United States of America

First Warner Books Printing: November, 1983

10 9 8 7 6 5 4 3 2 1

Renegade #21

RIVER
OF
REVENGE

El Generale Hernan Portola, Liberator of the South, or Butcher of León, depending on whom one asked, stood in uffish thought atop a pile of coral block rubble as he regarded a scene of almost total devastation.

According to the ordnance map of Nicaragua, there was supposed to be an old Spanish fort here. According to one's own senses, there was only a flat plain of shattered masonry and glass that smelled just awful. The sea-scented trade winds from the Mosquito Coast to the east helped a little. But the sickly sweet stench of death and the acrid reek of detonated high explosives still clung to the razed fortifications.

El Generale's men poked here and there amid the chalky rubble in hopes of salvagable weaponry. An army on the march needed all the spare parts it could find. As they moved about, wispy clouds of buzzing blow flies rose like smoke from where they'd been feeding—on charred lumps of human flesh, embedded like raisins in the debris. The soldados wore damp kerchiefs over their faces. It didn't really help. But orders were orders, and when one marched with El Generale Portola, one expected to smell death.

A pair of junior officers approached El Generale across the razed ruins. They marched in step, waist-high in flies, until they stopped, within easy conversational distance, saluted, and hit a brace as one.

El Generale stared down at them without expression as he asked, ''Well?''

His senior aide answered, ''We have spoken to the Indios in the village to the south, as you commanded, El Generale. As we suspected, it was the work of that Yanqui maniac, Captain Gringo. Los Indios say they were most grateful he warned them in time to escape the explosion here. They say they all ran well clear in time, and it only took them a day or so to put new thatch roofing on their miserable shacks.''

El Generale stared pensively out across the ruins for a moment before he observed, ''It's a waste of time for our muchachos to poke through the ruins for salvage, if those miserable Mosquito Indians have had all this time to pick over the rubble. On the other hand, it keeps the troops from plotting mischief if one keeps them busy.''

He turned back to his aides with a slight frown and added, ''So, the renegade, Ricardo Walker, is responsible for this mess as well as the carnage a good day's march to the west, eh?''

The senior aide said, ''Sí, my generale. As we figured his latest rampage, Captain Gringo and that loco little Frenchman he rampages with wiped out a whole column of guerrillas on our side, another column of guerrillas fighting for the *other* side, then shot up a river steamer before marching over here and blowing up all these European gunrunners.''

The other aide pointed out across the ruins and said, ''The Indios say he did this all by himself, without the help of even the loco little Frenchman! In God's truth, I have heard of homicidal lunatics in my time, but this one seems a one-man Horde of Attila!''

El Generale nodded thoughtfully and said, ''He certainly did a job on this place, and you say he did it all by himself? Madre de Dios, what manner of man can this Captain Gringo be?''

The less excitable aide shrugged and said, ''He is supposed to be a dead man, my generale. They keep trying to kill him. Yet he lives. It is said he became a Yanqui renegade when the Yanqui army court-martialed him and sentenced him for to hang. It is said the Mexican rurales tried to execute him too, when he escaped across the border from los Yanquis. Since then he has bounced all over Latin America as a soldado of fortune and most hot potato. Naturally, responsible people like ourselves wish to see him dead. But, the lousy pobrecitos who do not see the advantages of sensible government tend to lie to us about his whereabouts and . . .''

''Silencio!'' El Generale cut in with an imperious gesture, adding, ''I am not interested in the soldado of fortune's biography. I wish for to know his whereabouts at this moment. Did any of those Indios say they knew which way the Yanqui and his French associate went after blowing up this place, or do we have to beat it out of them the hard way?''

The senior aide shook his head with a smile and replied, ''We already pointed out the advantages of behaving as public-spirited citizens of Nicaragua, my generale. In truth, more than one seemed somewhat displeased at the ringing Captain Gringo left in everyone's ears as he left. They say Captain Gringo, the Frenchman, and their harem of adelitas left for that British navy base at Greytown, just down the coast.''

The other aide shrugged and said, ''By now they will have made it. It's been several days since they destroyed this gunrunners' nest. I don't know why, but our central government won't let us invade that damned British colony squatting on Nicaraguan soil.''

El Generale said, ''We're working with Washington on

that. Meanwhile, there are many ways to skin the cat, no? Captain Gringo and his friends could not have been invited to Greytown by Queen Victoria. So if he is in Greytown, it is as an illegal visitor the British do not know they have. I see no reason why two or more can't play the same game, do you? I need a couple of volunteers, muchachos. You, and you, will don civilian clothing and pay a visit on this Captain Gringo for me, no?''

The two aides exchanged glances. The more sensible one said, ''We shall arrange the matter at once, my generale. I see no difficulty in slipping into Greytown disguised as what the British tend to dismiss as mere natives. Finding a fellow tourist in Greytown may be more difficult. But rest assured, my generale, if he is there, we shall track him down and kill him for you as you wish!''

El Generale rolled his eyes heavenward and groaned, ''Listen to them, God! Am I really the only officer in this army You created with enough sense to unbutton his pants before he takes a piss?''

He glared down at his subordinates and roared, ''Idiots! Captain Gringo has left Nicaraguan soil after proving to everyone with the brains of a mosquito that it's suicide to tangle with him! He's obviously trying to get back to his hideout in Costa Rica, where he presents no danger to either side in our civil war. Yet you think I'm about to throw away even your miserable lives in an almost certainly futile assassination attempt?''

They stared, bemused, afraid to speak, since El Generale had obviously gone loca en la cabeza at the mere mention of the renegade's name. Finally one of the aides screwed up the courage to ask, ''If you do not wish the Yanqui dead, my generale, for why are you sending us to look for him?''

El Generale waved an expansive hand out across the rubble as he replied, ''To proposition him, of course. Look at the mess he made of this place all by his little self! Madre de Dios, I couldn't have done a better job with my whole army!

I don't want to kill Captain Gringo, muchachos, I want to *hire* the crazy bastard!''

The British protectorate of Greytown looked like someone had built a little bit of England, cheap, and marooned it on the Mosquito Coast.

The hotel Captain Gringo and his sidekick, Gaston, had checked into under false pretenses was pretending to be an English coaching inn that had somehow wandered into a mangrove swamp. The roofing was corrugated tin instead of thatch, and any paint they'd ever applied to the outside had been stripped by the muggy heat and constant trade winds. But at least the outside had weathered to a reasonably dry shade of silvery gray. It was more quaint inside. The wallpaper in Captain Gringo's corner room was fuzzy green with mold, and mushrooms sprouting from the rug in one corner. The brass bedstead, despite the smell of polish, was cheap-wedding-ring green in the cracks, and the room had cross-ventilation.

Gaston had said it was one of the better hotels in town. Captain Gringo didn't want to think what conditions in the native quarter could be like. As old hands at the knockaround life, the two adventurers had ditched the native girls they'd started out with and checked in here as a pair of traveling banana brokers from New Orleans. It didn't really matter if the management believed that, as long as their money held out. Gaston was out trying to scout up passage down the coast in his usual furtive gray way. So the tall blond American lay, hot, sticky, nude, and bored, across the fresh but already wilting linens on the bed, smoking a claro as he studied the ceiling. He was trying to decide whether the cracks in the plaster looked more like a map of Africa or of South America. He had decided it didn't really matter by the time he heard a discreet rap on the door across the room. It wasn't Gaston's rap. It was too polite to be a cop out there in the hall. So he guessed it was the maid. He got up, wrapped a towel around his middle, pulled his double-action .38 from its shoulder rig draped over a chair near the bed, and moved over to ask, "Yeah?"

A feminine voice replied from the other side, "I have to speak with you, Captain Gringo."

He didn't answer as he thought about that. The hotel help hadn't gotten his professional title from anything he'd signed downstairs.

He moved to one side and unlatched the door as he said, "Come right in." So she did, as he shoved the muzzle of his .38 against her ribs and slammed the door shut behind her with his bare heel, saying, "Don't turn around. Walk over to the bed and put both your hands on the brass. If you know who I am, you must know the form, toots."

His feminine visitor protested, "This is silly!" but did as anyone else with a .38 poking them in the ribs would do. As she moved to the foot of the bed and clasped the rail with both hands, he saw that she was a strawberry blonde with a silly little straw boater perched atop her pinned-up hair. She filled her Gibson Girl summer outfit—a thin white blouse and khaki whipcord skirt—rather nicely. She wore her skirt "Rainy Susie"—an inch or so higher around the ankles of her high-button buff kid shoes than Queen Victoria might have approved. He said, "Okay, move your feet back and spread 'em."

She did, but protested. "I'm off balance, you mean thing."

He said, "That's the general idea," as he started patting her down with his free hand. Up until then, he'd been using said hand to hold the towel around his waist. But modesty was less important to a man with a price on his head than making sure nobody figured to collect it. So as he searched her, standing behind her, he was nude. As he made sure she wasn't packing a rod between her thighs, she gasped, "My God, that's *me* you're grabbing there, Captain Gringo!"

He grinned and stepped back, saying, "Okay, only one of us has a gun. Just let me get my towel back and . . ."

She turned before he bent to pick up the towel. She was pretty as hell, considering the startled expression on her face when she saw what else he was pointing at her.

He laughed, picked up the towel, and said, "Sorry about that. Feeling pretty ladies up always does that to the little basser. Sit down, if you like, and tell me what the pitch is, miss, ah . . . ?"

"I'm Gloria. Last names don't matter, in my line of work."

"Oh? What kind of work are you in, Gloria? It's only fair to warn you I'm too romantic-natured to pay, no matter what you just noticed before I got this towel back in place."

She lowered her lashes with a becoming blush and said, "I know all about your reputation as a lover, Captain Gringo. That's not what I came to see you about."

"Oh, hell, it's starting to cool off a little, too. Okay, you're not a hooker and you're too pretty to be a house detective. But you keep using my name in vain. Who sent you, Gloria?"

"I'm, ah, not at liberty to tell you just yet. Do you have anything to drink? It's true that the trades are picking up now that the sun's moved to a less beastly angle, but it's still bloody hot and I'm perishing with thirst."

He nodded and moved to the dresser where he'd left the water olla, rum, and hotel tumblers. He could see her in the mirror, so he put the gun down. And still needed two hands to mix drinks, so he let go of the towel again. As it fell, exposing his bare buttocks, she repressed a smile and asked, "Do you often pose for sculptures, Captain Gringo? I mean, you do have a nice body, as well you know, but really . . ."

"What can I tell you, Gloria? I can see by your outfit that you're an old tropic hand, so don't try to tell me you don't lay around in the buff during la siesta, too."

She fluttered her lashes at his bare ass and replied, "Of course, but I almost always dress for company!"

"I wasn't expecting company. You want water with a little

rum or rum with a little water, Gloria? I used to have some ice, but not since I found myself south of Mexico."

"We British don't share your Yankee madness for ice. Make mind half and half, please."

He did. It was a point in her favor that she admitted being a Brit. He'd picked up on her educated English accent already, of course, but some dames lied even when the truth was in their favor. She was dressed sort of Yank, or at any rate more like American girls dressed in hot weather. He picked up the tumblers, thought about the towel on the rug at his feet, and wondered what the hell he had to hide that she hadn't already seen. So he just turned around and walked over to the bed with the booze.

She politely avoided looking down as she accepted her drink with a nod of thanks. He decided he'd look less naked sitting beside her than on the chair across from her. She repressed a flinch as he sat beside her, raised his own tumbler, and said, "Mud in your eye."

He let her take a good belt before he said, "Okay, are we going to get drunk or did you have a tale to tell me, Gloria?"

She took another sip of her drink and said, "Let's start by telking about *you*, Captain Gringo, alias Dick Walker. We know about the naughty things you just did up the coast, and we heartily approve. Both sides in that silly civil war are a bore."

"I found them sort of tedious. Who's *we*?"

"I'm not finished, Dick. At the moment your little French friend, Gaston Verrier, is under observation. Don't get excited. He's in no danger. I only mention him because you ought to know he's not going to be able to book passage out in the near future. It's the hurricane season and only the bigger steamers will be putting out to sea, for important reasons."

As if to prove her point, something tapped on the tin roof above like a ball-peen hammer. She blinked and asked, "Good Lord, what's that?"

He got to his feet and walked naked to the window to hold his glass of tepid rum and water outside as he said, "Hail.

Looks like we're in for a real thunderbuster. Sure you don't want some ice in your glass?''

She sniffed primly and said, "No, thank you. Do you have to expose yourself like that?''

He let a few hailstones plop into his drink as he replied, "I'm not exposed to anyone outside. If you don't like the way I dress in the privacy of my own digs, you can always leave. It's too hot to argue about formal attire, damm it.''

"Well, for heaven's sake, sit down again and stop waving that . . . you know, around. Be serious, Dick. I have important business to discuss with you.''

He sat back down beside her, tasted the drink, and said, "Not bad. Okay, let's get to the good parts. Who sent you and who do they want Gaston and me to shoot up?''

The hail was really coming down now. It sounded like a couple of skeletons were making mad gypsy love on the roof, using a tin can for a rubber. Gloria raised her voice and almost shouted, "Lean closer, damm it. I don't want the whole hotel to hear this.''

He moved until his bare hip was against her skirt, but said, "Don't worry, doll. The way it's hailing, we couldn't be overheard if your husband was under the bed.''

She laughed, unbuttoned her collar, and said, "I can't understand how it can be so bloody hot with ice bouncing off the roof! Would you mind if I, ah, got a bit more comfortable?''

He reached up, unpinned her straw boater, and said, "Hey, you can strip to the buff for all I care. When in Rome and all that rot, right?''

"Down, boy! I only mean to, ah, loosen up a bit," she warned, as she took another healthy swig of rum and water. He went on unbuttoning her blouse. The rum seemed to be loosening her up pretty good, but it was still hot and muggy in the room. She either didn't notice or didn't care as she said, "The people I work for don't want you to do anything particularly violent, Dick. It's a straight security job for an, ah, international trust; and speaking of trust, that's all the buttons I think we'd best unbutton until we know each other a lot better, dear.''

He'd already known from having patted her down that she was too smart to wear underwear on a tropical afternoon. So he stopped undressing her and didn't comment on the perky pink nipple peeking out at him from her open blouse as he asked, ''Where is the job, and, again, who's paying to have it done?''

''The engineering works you'll be guarding is up the San Juan, about halfway to Lake Nicaragua, Dick. There's been a little, ah, trouble with the natives. But if you were there with a machine gun or two . . .''

''Stop right there!'' he cut in with a frown. The hail pounded hard enough almost to drown him out when he continued, ''Trouble is all they grow in Nicaragua, and we're not about to go back for more, doll!''

She had to lean closer to be heard as she insisted, ''It's not in the war zone, Dick. My company has paid off both Granada and León, so no regular troops from either side will bother you!''

''Screw the regular troops. Have you heard about the guerrillas? Half the idiots running around with guns in Nicaragua these days don't know or care which side they're supposed to be on! But let's talk some more about your so-called natives. Are you talking about Indians or just old-fashioned peones? I don't like fighting either, Gloria. So far, the only good guys I've met in these parts have been poor barefoot boys trying to survive.''

She took another drink from her tumbler, held it out empty, and, as he rose to refill it, shouted, ''You're not listening, Dick! Nobody wants you and Gaston to fight anybody! Your job will be simply to guard the dam site. The workers you'll be protecting are as poor and doubtless as noble as Don Quixote might wish.''

He rejoined her, handed her the stronger drink he'd mixed, and said, ''Let me help you out of that blouse. The only things you have to hide under it are sticking out anyway, so why should the rest of you be hot and sweaty?''

She didn't resist as he peeled her to the waist, but lowered her drink to blink owlishly at him and observe, "You must be trying to get me drunk. I'm sure the queen would never approve of this, but, God, that does feel ever so much better!''

"Told you it would. Why don't we slip off that heavy skirt while we're at it, doll?''

"Oh, I couldn't. I'm not wearing anything under it, Dick!''

"That's a lie. You're wearing shoes and socks, right?''

She started to laugh. She couldn't stop, even when he kissed her. So he took her now half-empty glass, set it aside, and lowered her to her back across the mattress as he went on kissing her while he unbuttoned the waistband of her skirt. She kissed back with considerable enthusiasm, but when they came up for air the blonde protested, "Stop it, you naughty thing! Are you trying to seduce me, Dick?''

He slipped his free hand inside the loose waistband of her skirt, slid it down her bare belly to home plate, and, as he started massaging her clit, explained, "No, I think you came in here to seduce me. But what the hell, I can be a good sport if they send a really pretty dame.''

She gasped, grabbed his wrist, and made a gesture of trying to remove his hand from her privates. But she didn't really put her back into the effort as she sobbed, "This isn't fair! You're asking advantage of the heat and humidity to . . . Oh, God, let me get this perishing skirt out of the way so we can do it right!''

They did. He saw she was blond all over as he stripped her to only her high-buttons and gartered silk stockings. Of course he'd had to let go his advantage long enough to slip the whipcord out of the way, so the dumb dame went through the motions of trying to cross her legs, and would have doubtless *said* something as dumb if he hadn't kissed her, hard, and massaged her pale thighs open in welcome. As he rolled into the saddle she smiled up at him and said weakly, "They warned me something like this would probably happen."

Then, as he entered her, her eyes opened wider. So did her thighs, as she added, "Oh, I'm so happy it did!"

They went deliciously crazy for a while as the hail beat on the tin roof above them and heat lightning commented on her hot love box when it contracted in orgasm on his thrusting shaft. The storm cooled the air a little, but not enough to keep them from getting pretty moist. When she said she was all sweaty and icky, he withdrew, rolled her over on her hands and knees, and proceeded to pound her from behind with his bare feet on the gluggy carpet, asking her if that felt better.

She giggled, arching her back to aim her pale rump up at him as he slid in and out of her blond thatch. She said it felt ever so much cooler that way, which was a lie, because she was taking him hot and deep. He came in her, hard, and she slid off weakly to roll onto her back, holding up one hand to grasp, "Enough! I surrender, dear. But can we dry off and get out breathing back to normal before we do it again?"

He said that sounded fair, and fumbled out a cigar and matches from his shirt before sitting beside her on the bed. The match didn't want to light at first, but he finally got it going, lit up, and leaned on one elbow next to her, saying, "Thank you, Lord. I was expecting a much duller afternoon. Now could we just have some evening breeze, for chrissake?"

She smiled wanly up at him and said, "I never thought it would be too hot to fuck, once I saw your lovely dong, Dick. But now that we're back to earth again, you *were* about to tell me you'd take the job, weren't you?"

He blew a smoke ring at her breast, neatly ringing the nipple, and said, "You were going to tell me who we'd be working for, Gloria."

She shrugged and answered "The company's called Consolidated Construction, Limited. As I said, it's an engineering firm."

"Okay, so who are *they* working for?"

She frowned up at him in apparent confusion and replied,

"What do you mean, who are they working for, dear? They're working for themselves, of course."

"Honey, nobody works for themselves. You say they want to build a dam somewhere. Okay, who are they building a dam for? You don't just send a mess of men and gear up a jungle river and pretend you're a beaver, you know. The jungle on either side of the San Juan belongs to *some* damn body! Are we talking about the Nicaraguan bank or the Costa Rican bank of the San Juan, Gloria?"

She started to fondle his sated shaft as she said, "Who cares? I think it must be on the Nicaraguan side of the border, since that's who they bribed for permission to start work. The dam's not to be built on the main channel of the San Juan. I think they're damming a tributary. Some rapid little stream running down from the hills just to the north. Speaking of rapid streams, darling, why don't you put out that silly cigar and fill my main channel some more?"

He laughed but went on smoking as he said, "We've got plenty of time for that, doll box. Business before pleasure, if your outfit's really serious about hiring a professional machine-gun team. You were about to tell me who they were building this dam for, remember?"

She stroked him harder, and with hardening results, as she replied, "I was? Honestly, darling, I have no idea how the small print of that construction contract might read. I only work for C.C., Limited. I'm what you might call a personnel manager."

"You're managing my person swell, babe. But you're still trying to sell me a pig in a poke."

"Oh, poke it in me and we'll talk about pigs later!"

She was taking an unfair advantage of him, he knew. But since she was hot as a two-dollar pistol, two could play at the same game. He deliberately took a deep drag of smoke, blew it down across her heaving torso, and insisted, "Business is business. Before I give you the business again, let's nail down a few lines of that fint print, doll box. I'll take your word that you don't know who your outfit's working for. But since you work for them, you ought to at least know who the fuck *they* are, right?''

"Oh, yes, fuck me right! It's a London firm. You can look it up. For God's sake, Dick you've hired out as a machine gunner for people who can't read or write! What's so bloody important about my company's mailing address? I'll give you one of their bloody business cards if you want to cable them about my credentials. But could we please make love again first? I'm ever so hot, now that it's beginning to cool off a bit in here!''

Despite what she was doing to his dong, he shook his head and said, "I hate to relight a good cigar once it's been snubbed out in a dank ashtray. What's your hurry, doll box? It's still broad daylight, or it would be if that fucking storm would only let up."

She started playing with herself as well as him as she replied, "I can't stay much longer. But I have to come again before I go! Let me get on top if the rest of you isn't up to it. I see *this* part of you has risen for a lady like a proper little gent!''

She jerked it to full attention and added, with a giggle, "Heavens, did I say *little*? Go on and smoke your old cigar, dear. I'll just huff and puff at this end."

He lay back to blow smoke rings at the ceiling as Gloria forked a silk-sheathed leg over his pelvis and settled onto his shaft with a moan of pleasure. It felt great to him, too. But as she threw her head back, eyes closed, and proceeded to play pony boy on his naked lap, Captain Gringo asked conversationally, "Where are you going from here? Back to tell on me to teacher?''

She murmured, "Yes; I'm meeting my superiors for dinner at my own hotel. Oh, that feels so loverly! Ah, you did say you were coming with us, didn't you, darling?''

He grinned and said, "You keep that up and I'm coming for sure! But I have to think about the rest of the deal. I never sign a contract in the dark. I used to, but I got screwed that way a few times, and I don't mean *this* kind of screwing!

Maybe if I met the guys you're fronting for. What hotel did you say you were staying at, honey?''

She didn't answer. With a wild, wicked laugh she slid off his erection and dropped to her knees on the carpet, spreading his thighs as she lowered her blond head to envelop his trembling love tool in her lush pursed lips. He blinked in surprise but hissed in pleasure as she started to give him a fantastic French lesson, taking it beyond her gagging point to grip the head between her tonsils, with the warm wet tip of her tongue teasing him at the root.

He did what any man would have done, and doubtless what she wanted him to. He lay back and enjoyed it. But even as he watched the part of her strawberry-blond hair bobbing up and down, and, in the mirror beyond, saw she was fingering herself to orgasm at the same time, Captain Gringo was man of the world enough to know why she was doing it. A lady could hardly answer questions with her mouth full. Ergo, she didn't want to tell him whom she'd be meeting at what hotel.

But what the hell, that was fair, since he had no intention of romping through the Nicaraguan jungles with her or anybody else in the near future. He and Gaston had left with both sides in the current civil war mad at them. To top things off, they'd wiped out a gang of international gunrunners before making their graceful but somewhat noisy exit. Nobody she could be working for could possibly pay enough to make it worth his while to visit Nicaragua for a while.

He came deep in her throat. She gulped and kept swallowing his hard-on, hard, keeping it that way as she strummed her old banjo with the wet fingers of her free hand. As he watched her in the mirror behind her, it inspired him for a rematch, despite the fact that he'd have been running low on ammo by now with a less athletic and/or attractive partner. He wanted more, but he was sated enough to think clearly, and so he couldn't help wondering whether British intelligence or his old pal Sir Basil Hakim, of Woodbine Arms, Ltd., had sicked her on him. Gloria was too pretty and too skilled to be merely an enthusiastic secretary for some bush-league construction company.

But obviously she wasn't going to tell him, and meanwhile he was about to fire again in her pretty bobbing head, so he thought it only polite to mention it.

She slid her lips down the full length of his erection, tightly pursed, then rose to leap aboard him right, doing a cancan-girl's split with her long silk-sheathed legs on either side as she took him to the base of his shaft in a now impossibly tight opening.

She fell forward, pressing her aroused nipples to his chest as he tried to move and found, since they were both almost there and she was literally milking him with her fantastic internal muscles, that he didn't have to. They came together. It felt so good they both nearly fainted. It was quite some time before he remembered he had been smoking in this bed and weakly looked around for his cigar.

It was burning where he'd let it fall on the sheets. Thanks to the damp, it had only burned a dime-size hole before he picked it up and tossed it out the window across her lovely naked derriere. He said, "To hell with smoking and enough of this foreplay. Let me get on top so we can do some serious fucking!"

She laughed and rolled off him. But then she sat up and said, "I have to go now. Save me some for later, darling. I'll try to get back before midnight, if you promise."

"What's to promise? You see any other strawberry blondes around here? Let's make it midnight for sure. By then I'll have had time to check with Gaston and eat something to regain my strength. Drink plenty of coffee with your dinner, doll box. You won't be getting much sleep tonight."

She started reaching for her clothes as she shook her head and said, "That's not what I meant, dear. If I'm to come back and be your tootsie-wootsie, you must promise me you'll take the other job I came to offer as well."

He frowned and said, "I didn't know we were discussing prices, Gloria. Okay, it's against my principles, but I guess you're worth a hundred a night if you throw in another blow-job.''

She gasped in indignation and snapped, ''Are you calling me a whore, you renegade hired gun-slick?''

He smiled thinly and replied, ''We don't have to establish what we are, babe. We just have to agree on our prices! Gaston and me expect five hundred to a thousand Yankee dollars a month, depending on the risk, with expenses and fringe benefits like blond pussy thrown in.''

She rose to her feet, tugging up her skirt and fastening it as she said, ''This blond pussy has no intention of treking into any jungle. But I'll tell my employers your asking price.''

She was still steamed, but managed a smile as she pinned on her hat and added, ''If we have a deal, I may forgive you when I come back tonight with their counteroffer. I suppose I may have approached you in a manner that could lead a gentleman to entertain evil thoughts about a lady's, ah, natural feelings, but . . .''

.Then, before she could finish, or he had to come up with a sensible reply, all hell broke loose outside.

For a dame who looked so ladylike with clothes on, Gloria ducked pretty good. He didn't have to tell her that was no hail on the roof they were listening to now, as he rolled out of bed, dashed to the dresser, and got his .38. She crawled under the bed as Captain Gringo rolled across it, topside, to get to the window, gun in hand, for a cautious look to see what all that gunfire outside was about.

He saw nothing but an empty street with hailstones bouncing like popcorn on the wet brick pavement. The storm was letting up. The clouds above were thinning, but since it was late in the day the light tended to even out. Everything was the same shade of fuzzy gray. Another pistol shot echoed in the distance, and in some other unseen corner of the universe a tinny English police whistle tweeted like an enraged sparrow.

Behind him, Gloria stuck her head out from under the bed and asked what was going on. He said, ''Gunfight. But not close enough for us to worry about. Gaston said this was a tough little seaport. The storm's letting up. Let me get some duds on and I'll escort you wherever."

Again the strawberry blonde proved she was a quick-thinking little broad. She slithered out from under the bed and ran for the door, saying, "I can make it, dear. I'd better do so before the streets are crawling with perishing constabulary."

He said, "Hey, wait." But she had the door open and was saying, "Wait for me by midnight. I'll come to you at midnight, though hell should bar the way!" Then she blew him a kiss and was gone.

He laughed and locked the door after her. Then he got dressed. Her point about cops responding in droves to those gunshots in the neighborhood had been well taken, and, aside from feeling dumb talking to cops in the altogether, he couldn't hide his shoulder rig under his jacket unless he had his pants on as well.

He'd just put himself together, noting that it felt better in dank linen now that it was cooling off, when he heard Gaston's familiar knock on the door. He opened up. Gaston came in, soaking wet, to pull his own .38 and start reloading it as he muttered, "Merde alors, Greytown used to be such a civilized little village, too."

"Was that you I just heard smoking it up?" Captain Gringo asked as he stared down at the smaller, older, dapper little Legion deserter.

Gaston Verrier was one of those nondescript, gray little men who tended to get lost in a crowd. When one studied him more closely, one could see why women still found him attractive. Which was just as well, since Gaston was the original dirty old man. Despite his size, the wiry little Frenchman was a deadly fighter and a damned professional soldier of fortune, too.

Gaston peeled off his wet jacket, reholstered his reloaded .38, and moved over to the dresser to build himself a heroic drink as he explained, "I was jumped by rogues as I was wending my weary way home to you, my child. I don't think they could have been business associates of any of the people I contacted earlier this afternoon. Who but rank novices in the art would approach a total stranger in an alley, armed only with clubs and knives, hein?"

Captain Gringo said, "Mix me one, too. Who was doing all the shooting I just heard, if you were jumped by a gang of bully boys without guns?"

"Sacreblue, I had to defend myself, non?"

"That was all *you*? I counted at least a dozen rounds, Gaston."

"Oui. After I put all five of them on the bricks with my first improvised fusillade, I of course reloaded to finish the cochons off properly."

"Jesus, you just gunned five wounded guys in cold blood, Gaston?"

"Mais non, I was très how you say pissed off at them, my idealistic youth. I learned as a boy on the streets of Paris to be neat. Les police can be so tedious when one leaves behind a messy scene, with total strangers moaning and groaning and saying who knows what about one's description and probably whereabouts, hein?"

As Gaston handed the taller American his drink, Captain Gringo sighed and said, "Well, nobody can say you ain't neat, Gaston. But for chrissake, we're hot as hell and this is a well-policed small town."

"My point exactly. I shall give you the bad news first. The more-professional rogues I spoke to along the waterfront this afternoon told me none of the usual coastal traders will be putting out to sea soon. The species of insects are très nervous about hurricane weather."

"I heard the same story. What's the *good* news?"

"Perhaps I spoke in haste. You may not like the deal, my old and rare picker of nits. But this afternoon as I was sipping cerveza with a lass of forty-odd summers at a discreet cantina I remembered of old, we were approached by a dealer of deals. A junior officer of the Nicaraguan army said to be winning, this season. I of course sent away my plans for the evening, since she was in truth not that good-looking and you know how women gossip."

Captain Gringo took a swallow of rum and said, "Get to the point, dammit. I swear to God, Gaston, if somebody asks you what time it is you tell them how to build a grandfather clock!"

Gaston sat down on a hardwood chair his wet pants couldn't hurt and sipped his own drink before answering, "One never knows when one may wish he knew how to build a grandfather clock, my hasty child. But to hold your short attention span, I shall sum it up à la brass tacks. El Generale Hernan Portola wants to hire us, with the usual paid expenses, and a bonus on satisfactory completion of the job. We will naturally be screwed on that point. But I said we wanted our first month's pay in advance if we took the job."

Captain Gringo frowned down at the Frenchman and growled, "You did, huh? Who the fuck is General Portola and does he know we once fought on the other side against him?"

To answer your confusion in order, my old and rare, Hernan Portola is a dedicated cocksucker. He would no doubt prefer to be called the Butcher of León. Either description fits as well. And, oui, he knows we once fought for the Granadines or so-called rebels. Apparently he admires the way we sank that government gunboat on Lake Nicaragua for the sons of the bitch who never paid us for doing so."

Captain Gringo sat on the bed, lit another smoke, and shook his head to marvel, "Boy, you take the cake, old buddy. Can't you see a trap when it's drooling at your balls?"

Gaston shrugged and said, "If I had not seen the très clumsy trap in that alley on my way home, we would not be billing and cooing at one another like this. You must learn to pay attention to your elders, Dick. I said Portola was a *dedicated* sucker of cocks. He is très brutal, utterly ruthless, and all in all a man one would not wish to invite to one's home for dinner. But he is a sincere patriot, or at least sincerely dedicated to his own Nicaraguan faction. For León and the so-called liberal party, Portola would butcher any number of babies and bayonet his mother with a rusty blade. But, unlike so many warlords of bananaland, Portola keeps his word and never changes sides."

Gaston took another sip and reached for his own cigar as he added, "I suppose someone must have dropped Portola on his head when he was an infant. But, whatever the reason, he is known to those in our profession as a man who can be trusted. El Generale never crosses one double unless one tries to do it to him first. After that, of course, one must recall why they dubbed him the Butcher of León, hein?"

Captain Gringo thought, shrugged, and said, "Well, we can't stay here much longer, and we could sure use new ID as well as the bucks. But I don't like the idea of machine gunning old comrades in arms, even if the other side didn't pay us in full that time."

Gaston chuckled fondly and said, "Oui, I got some good screwing in the rebel camp, too. Mais relax, my conscience-stricken child. Portola's man said they did have a machine gun for you to work with, as well as a cute little field gun for moi, if we can manhandle it into the rough country involved. We are not, however, being sent to fight our old friends of the Granada faction."

"Jesus, two sides ain't enough in a civil war?"

"Mais non, that would be barely interesting. By now the war would be over if it was only between Granada and León. León, as you know to your sorrow, has been backed by recognition, loans, and other good things, like guns, from your doubtless confused President Cleveland."

"Never mind why Washington keeps backing piss-pot dictatorships down here. I've given up trying to figure that one out. Who, aside from their official enemies, does the so-called Nicaraguan government want bumped off, and how come they have to send out for help? Doesn't El Generale Portola have an army of his own?"

Gaston nodded and said, "Oui, armed, as we know to our cost, by Washington. That is where the wheels within the wheels of the clock you don't wish to hear about get très sneaky. Queen Victoria as well as President Cleveland expect Portola and his government to make la nice-nice. So Portola would be très embarrassed if either caught him with his bloody hands in the cookies, non?''

''Damm it, Gaston . . .''

''Mon Dieu, I am speaking as swiftly as one can with rum and tobacco in one's mouth, Dick! Eh bien, Portola wants us to take out an engineering project, started by outside international interests with the approval of both Washington and London.''

''Oh boy! Consolidated Construction, Limited, and a dam site in the jungles north of the San Juan?''

It was Gaston's turn to look surprised. He asked, ''Have you unsuspected psychic powers, Dick? The officer I spoke to said the project was supposed to be a deep dark secret!''

''A little pussy told me. You finish your story first.''

''Eh bien. As you know, various international trusts like the Vanderbilt transport complex and the banana barons of New Orleans do business in these parts with little regard for the local governments, since who can say who the local government may be from one day to the next? The Panama project Washington is interested in to the south has bogged down in très fatigue negotiations and gunplay. Meanwhile, weather and revolutions permitting, the easiest way to move freight between the Atlantic and Pacific is across Nicaragua near the Costa Rican border, which is also a somewhat hazy matter from one war to the next. Shallow-draft steamboats and cross-country railroads, while doubtless profitable to the heirs of Commodore Vanderbilt, involve much loading and unloading even when one considers how little one pays a stevadore down here. The British engineering firm has contracted to improve navigation on the San Juan, and supply hydroelectric power as well, by damming one or more tributaries to ensure high water at all seasons, and so on. I confess, the details of vast hydraulic projects interest me as little as my grandfather clock interests you. Suffice it to say, El Generale Portola does not wish to see the projèct brought to fruition. Ergo, he wants the works destroyed and the foreigners driven out of his country. He can't do it openly with his army regulars, because their pay and ammunition is supplied by the very powers he wishes to drive out of his country, hein?''

Captain Gringo whistled softly and said, "You say he never deals from the bottom of the deck, Gaston?"

Gaston nodded and said, "The triple-titted baby raper is as honest as your Abe Lincoln, when it comes to his given word. But you see, neither the junta in León nor El Generale ever *agreed* to the big construction project on what they regard, with some logique, as their own soil. Nobody ever asked them. Polite notes to Washington and London have been ignored, since, after all, who reads Spanish in either case? So, voilà, the simple solution, as Portola sees it, is to have the project destroyed, no doubt by guerrillas, disgruntled natives, or who can say, when anyone asks, hein?"

Captain Gringo took a drag on his claro, exhaled wearily, and said, "The construction outfit knows something's up. Pour yourself another while I tell you my tale. You'll need it."

He filled Gaston in on Gloria's visit, leaving out some of the dirty parts and keeping it short and sweet. When he'd finished and rose to build himself another drink, Gaston nodded and said, "Eh bien, someone has been fibbing to us. Probably both sides."

Captain Gringo asked him what else was new, adding, "There's more to this than a dam in the middle of nowhere. The Nicaraguans shouldn't give a shit if all the outsiders want to do is improve navigation and make some electricity the country could use. The blonde refused to say who Consolidated Construction was building said dam for, and it sure can't be the Nicaraguan government we all know and love. Could it be a ploy of the Granada side?"

Gaston studied his glass thoughtfully as he mused aloud, "Merde alors, that makes even less sense, Dick. As we learned the hard way, fighting for them, the Granadines are très flat broke. They would not be, if any outside powers were willing to loan them the time of the day. So Granada could not afford a big engineering project even if they had any use for one. And they have no use for one. León controls all the main water and land routes now. The Granadines have been reduced to guerrillas in the hills here and there. Besides the obvious, Portola would have a good excuse to publicly oppose the engineering project if Granada had a finger in the pie, non?''

The storm had faded to an occasional distant rumble of thunder now, but it was starting to get darker. Captain Gringo walked over to switch on the overhead Edison bulb as he said, ''Okay, let's write off all six or eight sides as just plain nuts and forget it. Are you sure you checked out every cotton-picking tramp schooner, Gaston? If someone like old Esperanza were to come tooling down the coast in her *Nombre Nada . . .''*

''Mon Dieu, to be so young and sure of his luck once more!'' Gaston cut in, adding, ''Your big gunrunning girl friend is up the coast giving aid and comfort to Mexican rebels at the moment. I asked. But don't jerk off in frustration just yet. Did not the blonde say she was coming back for a second helping?''

Captain Gringo consulted his pocket watch and said, ''That's hours from now. Besides, I don't like her deal as well as I like Portola's, and his stinks! I think it's time to pack our bags and scoot, old buddy. Too many people know where we are right now, and if only *one* of them goes to the local law and mentions those reward posters out on us . . .''

''Oui, even though we don't have bags,'' Gaston cut in with a laugh, then added, ''Even traveling light, we would travel très wet if we ran for the trees in this adorable wet season. Since you read maps as well as I, I shall not fatigue you by pointing out that no matter which way we leave Greytown by land, we shall be crossing into Nicaraguan territory, non?''

"Okay, so most of it's uninhabited jungle, but how the hell far can we be from the Costa Rican border?"

"About thirty Yankee miles, as a crow might fly. Needless to say, we are not crows. So one must allow for mangrove swamps and other très fatigue detours through the dripping annoyances of the Mosquito Coast."

"Hell, let's do it, then! Legged-up soldados can easily make thirty miles in a night's forced march, right?"

"Wrong. I just said there were endless swamps and trackless jungles in the way, Dick. And once we get to the San Juan, how do we cross the thrice-accursed estuary? It's almost as wide as the Mississippi at the mouth!"

"We'll cross that bridge when we come to it. We can't stay here now. Either side figures to turn us in if we say no, and nobody but an asshole would say yes to working for either a mysterious bunch of sneaks or a piss-pot dictatorship out to double-cross its own backers! The dame will expect an answer by midnight. How long did Portola's guy give you?"

"I said I'd meet him later this evening at the same cantina, after talking it over with you. Why?"

Captain Gringo started checking out his money and ammo as he muttered, "Shit, that means we should have started at least an hour ago! I don't have to worry about bullshitting Gloria and her pals. Portola's man will figure the answer's no if we don't get back to him muy pronto!"

Gaston shrugged and said, "Try it this way. I return to the cantina. Maybe that same mujer of forty summers will be there, so I may kill two birds with the stone as I assure El Generale of our undying devotion and send the disguised officer back to him, hein?"

"What if he insists on us going back with him? What excuse could we give him for saying no?"

"Your blonde and my somewhat-gray-around-the-edges lass of forty-odd summers? I don't think he would but it, now that I ponder the sense of two wanted men lingering in a British police station when safety lies just at the end of a hand-in-hand stroll to El Generale's camp just over the border."

Captain Gringo nodded and said, "Okay, I've the where-withal for a couple of not-too-serious gunfights and maybe enough to bribe a ferryman or so and still get us up to San José, once we make Costa Rica. How are you for rent money, once we get there?"

Gaston shrugged and said, "Minor expenses are no prob-lem to one who learned at his mother's knee to say 'hands up.' But let us further consider your droll comments on gunfighting! That officer neglected to inform me just where in the jungle one might expect to meet El Generale, and the sucker of cocks travels with an *army*, Dick!"

"They usually do. Meanwhile, the storm's letting up. The streetlamps are going on. In a little while the locals will be out strolling the plaza to see if they can get laid tonight, and the more proper lime juicers will be waving dinner. So who's going to notice if we leave this light burning and sort of slip out the service entrance downstairs? You know the area better than me, so we'll leave the best route out of town up to you."

"Oh, merci beaucoup, since there *is* no best way to anywhere I'd like to go! Portola would doubtless be waiting astride the one main trade route inland. The path we came in by from the north only leads back to the très disgusting chaos we came here to escape. The south road leads only to a pleasant stroll among the banana groves before it peters out in a mangrove swamp."

Captain Gringo nodded and said, "Good. That's the one nobody should be expecting us to take."

"But, Dick, the damned south road does not lead anywhere!"

"That's what I just said. Let's go."

They never found out just where the south road ended. More police whistles were tweeting somewhere in the night as they moved down the alley behind the hotel. Gaston observed that Captain Gringo's blonde had most surely ratted on him to the constabulary as they dog-legged across a side street and into yet another north–south alley. Captain Gringo had just said that didn't make much sense when they heard the distant sound of pistols shots, and he added, "See what I mean? Don't be so egotistical, Gaston. We're not the only knockaround guys on the Mosquito Coast. Her Majesty's constabulary are sort of stuffy bastards, and the civil war has all sorts of people ducking into Greytown these days. Where does this alley lead?"

"Merde alors, how should I know? Before I met you, I used to walk the streets like a gentleman. I see no light at the end of this particular tunnel, ergo we are approaching a part of town that the powers that be do not find worthy of streetlamps."

They moved out the far end and found themselves on a crunchy cinder path with barely a sliver of light showing here and there from the ramshackle houses on either side. Gaston said, "Now this is my kind of town. I smell West Indian cooking. The neighborhood is dark in more than one way. Let me get my bearings and . . . Ah, oui, the wagon trace out to the soggy farmlands to the south is around that corner to our right."

A few minutes later, as they moved along a rutted cinder path little wider than an alley would have been in the lighter-complected parts of Greytown, Captain Gringo narrowly missed stepping in a deep puddle and asked, "Are you sure this is the main drag south?"

Gaston cursed in French. Then the moon broke through a patch of thinning storm clouds, and as Captain Gringo could see farther, he nodded and said, "Okay, it has to go someplace if it's lined with shade trees."

Gaston said, "Those are not trees planted for shade, my pampered child. The wagon trace was hacked through the usual jungle that grows all by its adorable self around here. I told you Greytown was small. Regard how we are already leaving the last native shacks in our wake. You may walk ahead of me to step on crocodiles with those big feet of yours. We should be wading in a swamp any moment now!"

That wasn't quite true. The wagon trace ran straight and more or less dry to the southwest, in line with the coast to their left. The moonlight was okay, and as they crossed an open patch with pepper fields on either side the visibility got even better. Gaston started to light a smoke. But Captain Gringo warned, "Not yet," as he gazed back toward Greytown to see if anyone was trailing them. Nobody was. Gaston snorted in disgust but put his cigar away again as he observed, "If anyone was trying to keep us from leaving town, we'd have walked into their ambush by now, non?"

Captan Gringo started to agree. Then he frowned and said, "Stand right where you are and hold the pose. I want to see something."

Gaston snorted again, removed his planter's hat, and held it across his chest in a respectful attitude as Captain Gringo moved fifty or sixty feet back the way they'd just come. Then he nodded and rejoined Gaston to explain, "You were just a blur from point-blank range. So we should still be invisible from that tree line to the southwest."

"So what, Dick? Were we expecting to meet a pair of lovely ladies of the evening in the woods?"

"I don't want to meet *anybody* in the woods. I think it's scouting time. If I was going to set up for anyone taking this trail out of town, that tree line ahead would be my first choice."

He cut due west through the pepper field, crunching pungent peppers and reasonably dry soil under his mosquito boots as Gaston tagged along, muttering, "Such a suspicious nature. Who would want to harm a pair of sweet kids like us, hein?"

"If I knew how many players were in the game, I might have chosen sides back there. Keep it down to a roar. We'll hit the tree line a hundred yards from the road and work back tippy-toe, okay?"

"Merde alors, teach your grandmother how to knit. I was très tippy-toe before you were born, you overgrown sneak!"

It worked pretty good. They made the trees, which turned

out to be coffee, with the red earth well cleared between the close-spaced trunks, and were able to drift silently as ghosts toward the road until they both spotted the back of someone dressed in peon white cotton and a big straw sombrero. Captain Gringo stopped and nudged Gaston. The Frenchman whispered, "I see him. That rifle across his knees would indicate he has not squatted there to take la crappe. Ah, over to his right, resting his derriere against a treetrunk . . . he has a gun, too."

Captain Gringo drew his .38. Gaston frowned and asked, "Have you thought the matter out, Dick? Such gentlemen of the road tend to grow in bunches. There will be more on the far side of the wagon trace, non?"

"Yeah. I only want those two. Don't use that fucking knife of yours. I want to talk to them first."

"Merde alors, about what? I can tell you what they are doing there. They are waiting for someone less prudent than us to wander across those open pepper fields into their most ordinaire ambush, non?"

"Maybe. They could be mere banditos. They could be working for someone with more on his or her mind. You take the one on the right and I'll pistol whip the other. Let's go."

That should have worked, but it didn't. The two soldiers of fortune fanned out to move in on their intended victims. Then a third ladrón, whom neither had spotted behind a tree, stepped into view, facing them, and started to say something about it getting late before he gasped, "Ay caramba!" and raised the pistol in his right hand to shoot Gaston.

So Captain Gringo shot him, then blew away the squatting ladrón as he was turning his way, rifle and all. While all this had been going on, Gaston had of course blown the sombrero and half the head off his own victim.

After that it got even noisier. The two soldiers of fortune had crabbed away from their own muzzle flashes and taken cover behind coffee-tree trunks as bullets hummed like angry hornets through spaces they'd once occupied. A long ragged row of white-clad figures flashed on and off by dappled moonlight shining down between the treetops as they charged more or less blindly, which would have been dumb against almost any two men firing from cover. It had even grimmer results against two of the deadliest gunslicks in Latin America. The only thing that saved the ones still on their feet after ten white-clad figures lay stark in the moonlight was that they'd fallen back in panic by the time the two adventurers had to stop and hastily reload.

Gaston whistled and started running the other way. Captain Gringo hesitated, muttered, "When he's right he's right," and followed, catching up on his longer legs to snap, "Cut right, back across the peppers. If they're up to another charge they'll move due west through the coffee."

"Must you explain the facts of life to a man old enough to be your proud papa?" Gaston snorted, suiting his deeds to his words as they broke cover together to dash out across open but dark distance. Neither spoke as they ran across the crunchy pepper plants. They were slightly winded and very sweaty by the time they made it to the hedgerow on the far side and hunkered down by unspoken accord to see how many guys were chasing them.

Nobody was. Gaston gasped for air and spat before he said, "Eh, bien, those were not the usual highwaymen. They fought too seriously. Have you ever had the feeling that someone does not like you, and you can't say why, Dick?"

"Yeah, ever since I crossed the Mexican border a million years ago. Does General Portola lead uniformed guys or guerrillas?"

"Those were not Nicaraguan army troops, Dick. Besides, why would Portola send an officer to alert us to his interest in us if all he wanted was our adorable asses?"

Captain Gringo rose and said, "You're right. The guy you met at the cantina could have just tailed you back to me and made boom-boom, or, hell, just turned us in to the British authorities. The constabulary would have turned us over to the Nicaraguan government they recognize. Let's move sort of northwest and see if we can pick up another trail before we fall in a ditch. Thank God the moon's out and almost full.''

They started working around the hedge-in whatever, as Gaston observed, ''If we assume Portola didn't set that ambush for us back there, how do you like your strawberry blonde, Dick?''

''I liked her a lot, in bed. But she won't work either. Same reasoning. Why should the guys who sent her set me up for a great lay and a lot of bullshit about meeting me at midnight?''

''True, neither of us would have been alerted had neither of us been approached by anyone. At the moment, we would both have been asleep, or at least in bed, back at that untidy little hotel.''

They walked on for a time. Then Captain Gringo said, ''Shit, it doesn't make sense even if you assume a *third* side!''

''There is a third side, Dick?''

''At least a third. Maybe more. All sorts of people could be interested in whether that engineering firm does it's job or not. But, assuming a third party doesn't want us working for either Portola or Consolidated Construction, what was that bullshit back there all about? We were holed up in that fire-trap hotel, as you just said. If they'd caught us off guard, about now, with all exits covered and a match applied most anywhere . . .''

Gaston cut in to say, ''That is how I would have done it. But we just proved they were rather bushy of the league. They may have known we were *not* off guard. Guessing which route we would take out of town would not call for genius, hein?''

''Not if the guys doing the planning knew we'd been alerted. But if we assume they weren't the ones who tipped us off that it was moving time . . .''

''Oui, they have a spy in one or more of the other camps. I am betting on the construction company being indiscreet. El Generale Portola follows the standard practice of shooting any suspicious characters within his greasy grasp. But your adorable strawberry blonde has been trying to recruit hired guns, and who can say how many, aside from you, she screwed and chewed the fat with, hein?''

Captain Gringo chuckled and said, ''She chews pretty good. That's probably the answer. Let's not worry about it. Let's just get the fuck out of here and let all the little wheels spin within all the little wheels while we line up something safer in good old San José.''

They found a goat path and followed it until it joined a more substantial east–west wagon trace. Captain Gringo swung onto it and headed west. Gaston asked him what the fuck he thought he was doing. The tall American said, ''We can't go the other way, damm it! It leads back to town, and by now Greytown's hot as a whore's pillow on payday, as far as we're concerned!''

''True, alas, but you are walking us into even hotter territory, Dick. This is the road to Nicaragua's current war zone!''

''Tell me something I don't already know. We gotta go *some* damned where, and I don't walk through mud too good. Remember that cuesta of high sandy ground running north and south in line with the coast, a few miles inland? Well, we can follow this trail until it tops the cuesta, then swing left and whoopy-skippy through the reasonably dry and thin palmetto growth along said cuesta.''

''You're going to get us killed. Any bandits or wild Indians who avoid regular roads tend to stroll the high ground, too!''

''Okay, have you got any better way south in mind?''

''Mais non. But you're still going to get us killed.''

The moon played peek-a-boo as the two soldiers of fortune followed the trade route west. Fortunately, this stretch had been surveyed by British road builders and ran straight across the treacherous swampy areas. They passed a lagoon of scummy fresh water, infested with mosquitoes being snapped at by giant frogs being snapped at by even bigger alligators. Then Captain Gringo spotted palm fronds against the moonlit sky ahead and said, "Palmetto, front and center. Looks like we made it."

He spoke too soon. As they followed the road up a barely noticeable grade and moved into thicker, drier growth, a bull's-eye lantern opened its shutter to shine its beam in their faces as, all around, they heard the dulcet tones of rifle bolts, latching lots of rounds in lots of chambers.

They froze in place, hands polite, as Gaston muttered, "I *said* you were going to get us killed, Dick."

A voice from somewhere near the spotlight covering them said, in the polite casual tone of a guy who knew he had the drop on you, "We have been expecting you, Señores Walker and Verrier. You will come with us, por favor. El Generale is waiting for you in his command tent."

"So you are the notorious Captain Gringo," said the fat man behind the combined field desk and map table as the two soldiers of fortune took their places across from him in the sling chairs indicated. So far, they still had their side arms, but that didn't mean much with Krag rifles trained on their backs. It was hot as hell in the kerosene-illuminated command tent of heavy doped canvas, so the Butcher of León looked more like a baker who'd put in a hard day at his ovens as he regarded them with no expression on his dark greasy face. The soldiers of fortune were sweating too, and only partly because of the heat. El Generale Hernan Portola was not a friendly-looking guy as he sat there wearing class-A khaki officer's uniform despite the steamroom atmosphere. He nodded curtly at Gaston and added, "The mountain artillery in my train is impractical, if the contours of this map mean anything."

The two involuntary guests leaned forward to stare down with assumed interest at the ordnance map on the plywood between them and the spider whose web they'd blundered into. It was upside down to them, and neither gave a shit anyway, but El Generale's eyes were starting to look even more suspicious as he mused aloud, "I must say I was not sure I'd have the pleasure of your company, señores. You know, of course, what happened to the agents I sent to contact you in Greytown?"

They didn't. So it was easy enough to look up at him again with expressions of puzzled innocence. El Generale still looked unconvinced as he explained, "When the men I sent to get you failed to contact me this evening as planned, I sent others to make discreet inquiries. They were unable to find you. They found out my original agents lay dead in the Greytown morgue. The British constabulary had just found them in an alley. Both had been shot in the back. So forgive me, I don't mean to pry, but how is a man in my position to be convinced of your, ah, sincerity?"

Captain Gringo smiled thinly and said, "Easy. We're *here*, aren't we?"

"True, but alone. The officers I sent to recruit you were to escort you here. But they lie dead in Greytown, while you two, forgive me, could have been going almost anywhere when my men intercepted you, no?"

Gaston laughed easily and said, "You would have to forgive me indeed, mon général, if I told you in detail what I think of your logique! Dick, here, never met either of your agents. I met one, it is true. I did not know he came in pairs. Like yourself, we wondered why he was not at the meeting place I'd arranged with him this afternoon. We heard some gunshots earlier. Until now we did not, I give you my word, connect them to anyone important to us. But with the police running about blowing whistles and no guides to show us the way, voilà, we came looking for you, and so here we are."

"*If* you were searching for this camp and not just trying to escape." Portola said flatly.

Captain Gringo made a mental note that he was smarter than he looked before he told the officer, "There are three or four ways out of Greytown. Anyone with half a brain could guess you'd be camped here on this dry cuesta, for Pete's sake.''

Gaston added, ''Mon Dieu, do we look stupid enough to assassinate two Nicaraguan officers and then charge blindly into their camp?''

Before Portola could think about that, Captain Gringo said, ''We had trouble in Greytown too. Some guys jumped Gaston, here, in an alley near our hotel. You can read about it in the papers, and your two officers were still alive at the time.''

Portola looked relieved and asked, ''Oh, were you the señores who left those bodies in that alley? That, at least, rings true. But who in the devil could *they* be working for?''

Captain Gringo said, ''Easy again. An outfit calling itself Consolidated Construction, Limited, sent a female agent to recruit us. You can see what our answer was. The mujer said she didn't want us working for you. She said they had us under observation. Obviously someone working for them was trailing Gaston when he met your agent in that cantina. What else do you need, a diagram on the blackboard, for chrissake?''

Apparently Portola did, but he drew the pattern in his own head as he let them sweat some more. After a while he nodded, slid a box of Havana perfectos across the map at them, and said, ''Bueno. I'm glad you chose the right side. We have Browning, Maxim, and Spandau machiee guns, all chambered for the same .30-30 rounds as our Krags. Which make do you prefer, Captain Gringo?''

''I'll stick with Maxim's original patent, since I trained on it. The Browning fires a little smoother, but it's sort of delicate for the local climate. The Spandau needs more work if the young kaiser expects to ever do anything important with all those Spandaus he's pirated from Maxim's original deiign.''

Gaston snorted in annoyance and cut in to ask, ''Is there some point to all this discussion of machine-gun patents, or does M'sieur le Général have some particular target in mind for les rat-a-tats?''

Portola stabbed a stubby finger down on the map, marking the target area with another grease spot as he said, ''The

British firm wishes for to dam this stream and flood this jungle valley. I do not wish for them to do so. For political reasons, I cannot make my displeasure publicly known. I am therefore obliged to send a guerrilla band, led by you professionals, to take out the damned foreigners.''

Captain Gringo said, ''We heard all that from your agent and the dame from the other side, general. What's the bottom line?''

Portola shrugged and said, ''I shall pay you a flat fee. Five thousand Yanqui, to share as you see fit, up front. You will get another five when I hear you have wiped the project out in a satisfactory manner.''

The two professionals exchanged thoughtful glances. Captain Gringo asked, ''What do you call a satisfactory wipe-out, general? No offense, but I'm not a butcher. So women, children, and unarmed peones are out.''

The Butcher of León shrugged and said, ''I don't care what you do to the work force, as long as I can rest assured that cursed dam will not be built in the near future. Do it neatly, or do it sloppy, but *do* it, and the bonus is yours. Agreed?''

Captain Gringo shook his head and said, ''Let's go over the fine print. If we're to stop the project to your satisfaction, we need some facts.''

''Let's talk about the money first!'' Gaston cut in.

Portola shrugged, reached in a drawer, and handed Gaston a check, saying, ''As you see, it's a cashier's check made out to bearer on a Costa Rican bank in San José. When you take out the dam site, you won't have to come back to me. In fact, I'd rather be able to say I didn't know either one of you, should anyone ever ask. There will be another check like that one waiting for you in San José if I am pleased with the results of your mission. If I am not you will die before you can cash either.''

Captain Gringo said, ''Let's stop trying to scare each other and get back to the brass tacks, general. Numero uno, who the fuck's paying to have all that construction work done in the first place? I asked the dame they sent to recruit us, but she either didn't know or wouldn't say."

Portola shrugged and replied, "Nobody ever saw fit to tell us why they needed a flood-control and hydroelectric project on that tributary, either. The official word they sold Washington and London was the usual tripe about improving living conditions for the probrecitos. They say they can improve navigation on the San Juan and set up a model village and industrial park on the riverbank as well."

"Do you think it's a cover for something more sinister?"

"Quien sabe? I don't care what they really intend. It's the *Mosquitoes* I'm worried about."

They both looked up. Gaston said, "The insects are très formidable at this time of the year, mon Général, but one would assume in time one could learn to live with a few mosquitoes, non?"

Portola shot him a disgusted look and said, "I am referring to the Mosquito *Indians*, damm it. We're already having enough trouble with the wilder tribes of our Mosquito Coast. And every time we have to shoot a few of the cabrónes, the triple-titted missionaries write more silly letters to the international press, accusing us of being uncivilized to our uncivilized minorities."

Gaston grinned and said, "Mon Dieu, how uncivilized of them! Everyone knows León is of the liberal party, non?"

Fortunately, Portola didn't understand Gaston's sardonic wit. He nodded soberly and replied, "Public opinion is a pain in the ass. But what are we to do? We depend on the fucking Protestants in Washington and London to back us against the fucking Pope and the Granadines. Everyone knows the only good Indian is a dead Indian, but the damned Calvinist missionaries and the even worse Dominicans on the damned Granada conservatives' side weep and wail as one, every time we have to shoot a damned Mosquito. You know, of course, how England used protecting the so-called oppressed Indians as an excuse to shove that base at Greytown down our throats. We don't want anything like that to happen again. So I'm sending you two cutthroats to take out that dam and make sure it *doesn't* see?''

Captain Gringo lit the perfecto he'd accepted while he tried to make some sense out of what the fat man had just said. It didn't work. He shook out the match and said, ''General, I don't know what in the hell you're talking about. What has building a dam in the middle of nowhere got to do with Mosquito Indians?''

''Where did you think wild Indians lived, in the middle of Granada or León? The foreigners building that dam against our wishes in the name of so-called progress take the same position about the jungle valley they intend to flood being worthless and uninhabited, but . . .''

''Gotcha!'' Captain Gringo cut in, adding, ''I must be asleep at the switch tonight. God knows I've met enough Indians out in the middle of nowhere. The dam project figures to flood their happy hunting ground, huh?''

''A couple of Mosquito villages and a thousand or more corn milpas too! You probably know los Mosquitoes are a slash-and-burn semiagricultural tribe. If they're flooded out, they'll move into the happy hunting grounds of other bands. That will mean intertribal warfare, and you may have noticed we Creoles have our *own* intertribal warfare to worry about right now! It gets even worse if the Indians attack the construction workers instead of other Indians, or us. Let Consolidated Constructions, Limited, send out a call for help to the Royal or American Marines and . . .''

''I said we understood your problem,'' Captain Gringo cut in, as Gaston just sat there bemused. The tall American went on, ''Smoking up the construction site with machine-gun fire would be the best way to call in outside help, general. What you want is a demolition job. The French canal builders down Panama way didn't give up because half their workers died of yellow jack. They went bust when they couldn't replace the heavy construction gear they were losing to flash floods and landslides.''

Portola nodded and said, ''We *do* think the same way, I

see! Bueno. I shall see you have all the dynamite your porters can carry.''

"We get *porters?* How about some *fighting* men, general?''

Portola frowned and said, ''If I wished any of my soldados seen anywhere near the dam site, we would not be having this conversation. You have my permission to arm your peones and give them some basic training as you lead them through the jungle, of course. I have a dozen more or less reliable pobrecitos I can volunteer for your mission. They, of course, will insist on bringing along their women. If the women carry most of the load and I issue your porters a few guns to go with their machetes . . .''

Gaston cut in to ask, ''Why can't we find a couple of stout m'selles to haul a Mountain 75 at least? Shoving la boom-boom under someone's derriere can be très fatigue. While lobbing H.E. from a safe distance can become the soup of a duck, hein?''

El Generale just looked disgusted. Captain Gringo pointed at the map with the tip of his perfecto and explained, ''When the contour lines get this close together, they're trying to tell you the slopes are damned near cliffs. I see . . . four, make it five really nasty ravines between here and there that I'm not sure we're going to get across, even with only our own bare asses to pack. Could I turn this thing around for a better look, general?''

Portola swung the plywood map table around on its lazy-Susan mount as an aide-de-camp ducked in, scowling. The tall American ignored him as he told Gaston, ''Okay, I can see where they'd put the dam between these two peaks. Assume the crest meets this twenty-meter contour line if they're talking about enough hydroelectric power to matter and . . . Boy, that's going to be one big lake where this valley full of Indians is supposed to be!''

The junior officer had been putting a bug in the general's ear while the soldiers of fortune were studying the layout. Portola's voice dropped sharply as he cut in, ''We have just learned that a patrol I sent out has been badly mauled. One squad wiped out. The others just made it back, carrying some wounded. I don't suppose you could tell us anything about that, either?''

Again, caught by surprise, Captain Gringo was able to meet Portola's cold suspicious eyes with an innocent stare as he replied, ''Don't look at *us*, general. The only patrol of yours that we ran into had the drop on us before we spotted them.''

Gaston had to ask, ''Where and when did the outrage occur, mon général?''

So Portola explained, ''When I heard the men I'd sent to contact you had been murdered, I naturally sent some men, in peon costume, to cover the escape route south of Greytown. I confess, at the time, I entertained doubtless groundless suspicions about your sincerity.''

The two soldiers of fortune exchanged glances. For once Gaston was smart enough to keep his trap shut as Portola added, ''Sí, they had set up an ambush south of Greytown. Fortunately for yourselves, you did not walk into it. Unfortunately for my muchachos, someone jumped them from behind and shot them up most severely.''

Captain Gringo smiled thinly, as Gaston studied the tip of his own cigar with sudden interest, and then, since someone had to say something, Captain Gringo said, ''No shit? Did your boys get a good look at the sons of bitches?''

Portola looked up at his aide, who shook his head and growled, ''The counterpatrol hit them from the dark in a coffee plantation. From the rapid fire they were subjected to, they feel sure they were jumped by at least a dozen hombres, armed with repeating weapons. Probably light carbines, judging from the flashes and reports.''

''Or one machine gun?'' asked Portola, staring hard at Captain Gringo.

That was so silly that the tall American was able to laugh sincerely before he replied, ''Feel free to search us for concealed machine guns, general. I can't prove we didn't check into that hotel in Greytown with no luggage, but you ought to have no trouble checking that out if you have pals in town. I like the lieutenant's theory about carbines better.''

Gaston snorted in dramatic disgust and chimed in, ''Merde alors, why are we having such a silly discussion? All of us are professional military geniuses. Any corporal would be able to tell us that one does not shoot up patrols with anything, unless one has a reason, hein? Let us assume for the sake of insane suspicion that two rude youths such as we jumped one of your patrols with our own squad of infantry, a mysterious machine gun, or, sacrebleu, our own two little pistols.''

''Did you?'' El Generale asked flatly.

Gaston grinned and said, ''Mais ouil We did it to clear our escape route south, as you suggest. Then, having done so, we came right out here to you to ask if you approved, non?''

Portola looked relieved and said, ''Bueno. Not even the mad and most unpredictable two of you have the reputation for total insanity. But *somebody* shot the pants off my muchachos and if I ever find out who it *was*...''

''How soon do you want us to leave for that dam site, general?'' Captain Gringo asked, to change the subject.

Portola said, ''You shall leave at first light. My men will show you to your tent, and I suggest you get plenty of rest before morning. The target area is a good sixty kilometers cross-country, and the country, as you just noted, is muy rudo. We can discuss your porters and the gear you will require in the morning. Forgive me, señores, but I have other matters to deal with here. The mission I am sending you on is but a side issue of our more important civil war.''

They rose, but Gaston said, ''Forgive me, M'sieur le Général, but we did not eat dinner this evening.''

Portola waved a hand in dismissal as he muttered something about the officer leading them out getting them some grub as well. Captain Gringo nudged his small hungry comrade and they followed the aide out into the darkness. Gaston protested softly, ''Merde alors, I am *hungry*, Dick!''

Captain Gringo didn't answer. He was hungry too, but they still had their guns, extra smokes, and their lives. So what the hell.

The aide led them silently to a tent down the line and ushered them inside rather sullenly. They saw that the tent was illuminated by a kerosene lamp and furnished with pallets on the ground canvas instead of folding cots. Their guide ducked back out with no further comment. They each flopped down on the bedding with the central tent pole between them, and when Gaston started to say something, Captain Gringo snapped his fingers and pointed at the thin canvas wall rising above him. Gaston nodded, blew a cloud of perfecto smoke, and said, "I told you what a nice man the great Portola was, Dick. Wasn't it nice of him to give us these formidable cigars?"

Captain Gringo shot him a disgusted look and said, "Yeah," in English, to make anyone listen work at it as he added, "I noticed that one of those hills they mean to plant one wing of the dam against is contoured like a Cheyenne lodge. Think it could be a volcano?"

"Hardly an active one, if they are professional engineers. But old cinder cones dot the landscape of Nicaragua très fatigue. It must have been a très smoky neighborhood when the world was younger, non?"

"Yeah. Negative on a cinder cone for a dam-foundation wing, though. The old volcano has to be solid basalt lava or the dam wouldn't hold. I noticed on the map that there's a good-sized crater topside."

"So what? That blonde they sent to tempt you from the straight and narrow Cause of León said her side was hiring guns too, non?"

Captain Gringo stubbed out his cigar in a tin ashtray provided by the management and mused aloud, "Right, that's where *I'd* have a lookout posted if I worked for C.C., Limited. That one fucking peak dominates the whole area, and we'll have to work close!"

"Eh bien, it's the rainy season and forest canopy covers

everything even when the view from a mountaintop is more reasonable down here. Damn, I wish I had something to eat. Next to going to bed alone, there is nothing that keeps me awake like going to bed on an empty stomach.''

Captain Gringo started to undress as he said, "Quit reminding me, damm it. Get some sleep while you can. Want the light out?''

"Mais non. I am not afraid of the dark, but some few species of insects are afraid of the light. I am not quite hungry enough to eat rat-sized tropical roaches, and I no longer find it amusing to wake up with a scorpion in my ear.''

Captain Gringo nodded and finished stripping. He made a pillow of his shirt and jacket and slipped the .38 under it before stretching out nude under one thin sheet.

Gaston had just done the same when the tent flap opened and two adelitas ducked in, giggling. Neither of the camp-following dames looked bad, but the really beautiful sight was the trays of refreshments they carried.

The one who'd seen Captain Gringo first dropped to her knees beside him, presenting the corn bread and chili con carne she'd brought as well as a carafe of red wine for his inspection. He propped himself up on one elbow and told her he loved her. She giggled and said she was called Dulcenita. He said she looked sweet to him, too, and dug into the grub. It was spiced enough to make most Anglos wince, but he was used to Latin cooking and hungry as a bitch wolf, so what the hell. If he washed it down with the dry peon wine, it probably wouldn't detonate in his guts. Dulcenita seemed to be hanging around for something. He knew you had to be careful about offering tips anywhere but in a cantina. So he asked her if she'd like some wine.

She giggled, took a swallow, and said, "El señor is trying for to get me drunk, no?''

He said she could get as drunk as she liked. Then, catching sight of what Gaston was doing to his own waitress across the tent, he added, "Hey, Gaston, for chrissake, these dames could belong to somebody with a gun!''

Gaston murmured something in the ear of the one he'd been feeling up, and as she rose to snuff the lamp, he said, "I most naturally ask about such things before I slip my hand under any skirt, my prim and prudish schoolboy!"

As the tent was plunged in darkness, Captain Gringo growled, "Jesus H. Christ, if I get any of this chili in my eye it'll never heal! Couldn't you have waited until we finished eating, you old fart?"

"Mais non; I eat lightly, when I anticipate a grand dessert. Excuse me, Dick, I can't talk to you right now. I seem to have a tit in my mouth."

Captain Gringo laughed, shoved the tray up against the tent wall where the bugs could get at it without crawling over him in the dark, and reached for the wine Dulcenita had been holding when the lights went out. As his hand landed in her lap, he didn't find himself grabbing a drink. The little adelita had pulled her skirt off over her head, and, like most Indian or half-Indian girls down here, she'd either shaved or plucked the fuzz from around her snatch.

She laughed and climbed on top of him as he held on to his advantage. Dulcenita whipped the sheet from between them and forked a firm, chunky thigh across him to settle on his semierection before he'd had time to really get hot. As her warm wet flesh enveloped him he rose to the occasion as any gentleman would, of course. Dulcenita lowered herself gingerly, gasped, and said something in her Indian dialect to her unseen companion across the tent. From the answer she received, one could tell she was forced to speak with her mouth full. So Captain Gringo's bedmate laughed and started moving up and down, taking it deeper with each stroke as she got used to the unexpected blessings she was receiving.

He reached up to fondle her topworks, noting with mild surprise that she still had her blouse on. It was odd how working-class American and Latin American girls shared the same odd shyness about total nudity in bed, even though they screwed everyone they knew, if asked at all politely. As a Mosquito or at best a backwoods mestiza, he knew she probably didn't know how to kiss, either. But she sure knew how to move her broad brown ass.

He let her bring him to climax. It was still hot and muggy. But he wasn't even sweating as she milked his first discharge out of him and kept going. He ran his hands up under her blouse. Her breasts were filmed with her own perspiring efforts and he could tell she was getting there herself. He suggested taking everything off. Dulcenita murmured, "Oh, no, por favor, only wicked girls allow men to see them naked, señor!"

"Call me Dick. I can't see a fucking thing in this darkness, querida, and, speaking of fucking . . ."

He rolled her over on her back without withdrawing and pulled her blouse up to expose her sweat-slicked breasts to his own heaving chest as he proceeded to do it right. She moaned in pleasure and said, "Oh, Deek, you are so thoughtful. This feels so much nicer for me. But are you sure you do not mind my enjoying you so selfishly?"

He shoved her blouse off over her head as she started to protest, then wrapped her soft plump arms around him and sighed, "You are right. It does feel even better this way. But please don't tell anyone I took all my clothes off. I have my reputation to consider!"

He kissed her to shut her up as he pounded her to glory. She kissed at first like a little girl, or an Indian. Then, as he felt she was starting to climax and parted her pursed lush lips with his tongue, Dulcenita showed she was willing to experiment and a willing pupil. She sucked his tongue almost out by the roots as she locked her strong legs around his waist and tried to pull what she had in that end out by the roots as well.

He was still inspired, very inspired, when she went limp in his arms and lay quietly pulsing in postclimactic contractions until she realized he wasn't even slowing down. She gasped something in her Indian dialect, and the unseen girl with Gaston giggled and said something back that sounded dirty, even when you couldn't understand it. Gaston growled in

English, "Can't you two make love without distracting conversation? I am trying to teach this adorable child how we do it in Paris with our, ah, best friends."

Captain Gringo laughed and said, "Kiss it once for me. I don't know what the fuck they're talking about. But we both seem to be doing something right."

The conversation had distracted him as well, so he had to start over to catch up with his own bedmate. She murmured, "Wait. My friend, Rosa, says she has just discovered a new way to please a man. Roll on your back, my toro. I wish for to see what she finds so amusing about this French business."

That sounded fair. So Captain Gringo rolled off, albeit halfway to the edge and sort of anxious as Dulcenita groped for his erection in the dark, then lowered her head until her long black hair was sweeping his naked belly, and proceeded to act French indeed.

As she started blowing the charge on his bugle, Captain Gringo chuckled and muttered in English, "I'll be damned. I think they're playing follow the leader!"

Gaston replied, "Oui; now aren't you glad you teamed up with a man of my vast experience? What do you suggest I suggest next for Rosa here? She seems the eldest and more willing pupil, and I fear the ruffians they usually service know nothing about the subtle ways to enjoy a woman, hein?"

Captain Gringo didn't answer. He was coming. He grabbed Dulcenita's well-lubricated crotch in the dark and encouraged her flute solo by massaging her wet clit with one hand as he ravaged the rest of her goodies with the other. She went nuts on his shaft and took it deep throat while he tickled her, finger-fucked her, and got a pinkie up her winking anus so it wouldn't feel left out. As he fed her his wad he could tell from her pulsations that she was coming too. She fell limply on her side with a thigh across his chest and proceeded to give a blow-by-blow description of what they'd just done to her pal across the tent. As Rosa responded by following the leader, Gaston sighed, "Oh, thank you, Dick! I'll never forget what a friend you've been tonight!"

Captain Gringo woke up with a start, reached for his .38, and relaxed as he realized he'd been awakened by the distant sounds of pots and pans. He was alone atop his rumpled bedding. He didn't worry about that, either. He muttered, "Hey, Gaston?" and when the Frenchman answered in a sleepy voice, he added, "I think it's getting dawnish outside. Someone's cooking breakfast up the line. Can you see what time it is?"

"Merde alors, you have the watch, and it's still pitch black in here. Go back to sleep, you species of early bird-life. They shall blow a bugle when El Generale wants everybody up, you idiot!"

That sounded sensible. Captain Gringo lay back down, albeit now wide awake. The chili concarne was repeating on him. He groped out some matches and found the stub of the perfecto he'd stubbed in the tin ashtray before turning in. It only tasted like shit for the first few puffs. Then the good tobacco took over from the overnight mildew.

The tent flap opened, exposing a flash of dismal gray light as the girls came back in with hot coffee and tortillas, bless their little hearts. He sat up and groped for the breakfast Dulcenita had brought him. She sat giggling while he consumed it. Then, feeling better, he groped for Dulcenita for dessert. Only, it wasn't Dulcenita, as he discoveed when he laid her across the bedding to undress her again. Great minds running in the same channels, Gaston observed, "Excuse me, Dick, do you have Rosa over there?"

"I think so. Want to swap?"

"Mais non; but I think *they* do. Shame on you, Dick, this one is built like a little girl and . . . Mon Dieu, who taught her to grab a man's foundations with such a firm hand?"

Captain Gringo laughed and didn't answer as he explored

the surprise in his own bedding with his own hands. Rosa was
built much bigger and softer. He didn't kiss her lips. None of
them had had a bath since the two girls had played follow the
leader on everyone's dongs a few hours ago. But as he
explored between her soft fingers, he could feel she'd at least
dunked her crotch in a nearby creek, so what the hell. He
could tell because her lap, unlike Dulcenita's, was well
thatched with thick moist pubic hair. Everything else about
her was a novel challenge too. So he rolled into the saddle of
her welcoming raised thighs and said, "Oh, yeah!" as he
sank into a totally new experience.

Rosa was softer, looser, warmer, and more experienced
than the one he'd had before. She moved great and he forgave
her for being built bigger when she contracted with skill on
his questing shaft and bounced so good he hardly had to do
any work. Their upper torsos fit nicely together. He could lay
more weight on her big soft breasts without worrying about
her comfort. Considering what the two of them had put him
and Gaston through only a little while ago, he was able to
come in her fast. He could tell she enjoyed novelty too.

But when she whispered further suggestions, nibbling his
ear lobe as they relaxed in each other's arms, he said, "I
think we'd better quit while we're ahead, querida."

Somewhere a tinny bugle sounded. He sighed and said,
"See what I mean?"

"Put it up my ass at least once," Rosa pleaded, adding,
"You did it to Dulcenita, no?"

He laughed, dismounted, and wiped himself off before
groping for his duds and insisting, "Later. There's a general
who might want to screw us, too. Are you girls coming on
the expedition with us and the others?"

Rosa pouted and said, "No. We are attached to the mess
staff. And they say the odds are against either of you nice
boys ever coming back alive. It's not fair. Dulcenita got to
take it in her ass and mouth with you and I'll probably never
see you again."

"Well, look at it this way, you're ahead of her with

Gaston's dong, so it ought to even out. Are you getting dressed, Gaston?''

"In a minute. At the moment I am giving this adorable child a Greek lesson."

"You see?" sobbed Rosa, swiveling around on her knees to shove her broad derriere almost in Captain Gringo's face. He had his shirt on already. But he wanted to leave her with fond memories of them both. So he laughed, rose to his knees, and rubbed his semierection in the moist groove between her buttocks until it was hard enough to go almost anywhere. He said, "Lady's choice," and Rosa took the matter firmly in hand to work her tight rectal opening over the head, gasping, "Oh, wait, what am I getting into me?"

"Maybe we'd better settle for doggy-style, eh?"

"No, hold still, and let me get used to this. . . . Oh, my God, are you sure Dulcenita took you this way, Deek?"

"I never said she did."

"Well, *she* did!" Rosa gasped, pushing back with a determined grunt of mingled discomfort and dawning interest until it was well up her rear and she was able to take his first gentle thrusts. He asked how it felt and she said, "Just *do* it!" before switching to her own dialect to jeer at the giggling girl with Gaston. Then, as the tall American began to get interested enough to move faster, Rosa laughed lewdly and explained, "I caught her in a lie. Bueno. Now I, Rosa, am the only one who can say I took you *both* in the ass, no?"

Across the tent, Dulcenita protested, "Pooh, I have just taken Señor Gaston so, and I sucked them both besides, so there!"

Captain Gringo let himself go, to satisfy Rosa's boast and his own horny nature. Then he wiped off carefully and hauled his pants and boots on before either of the adelitas could show off anymore.

He noticed Gaston walking sort of funny too as they went outside to see what else was up. The sky was gray as the belly of a big dirty sheep and the whole world looked fuzzy and damp. They didn't bitch. They both knew that by noon they'd be either sunbaked or under a cold shower with their clothes on. The only time the temperature was reasonable this far south was when it was dark or overcast but not raining.

They notice a commotion down the line and drifted that way, ignored by the few soldados moving up and down the tent rows on their own camp chores.

The fuss was taking place just beyond the command tent. The general wasn't in sight. That made sense, when you thought about it. Nobody fussed at generals. A junior officer and a senior noncom were arguing loudly while others stood around rooting for one side or the other. As the two soldiers of fortune approached, the sergeant was protesting, "For why must I leave my mujer behind in camp? By the beard of Christ, she is no mere adelita. We are married in the eyes of the Church as well as in the eyes of God, lieutenant!"

The officer, the same young sullen guy who'd led Captain Gringo and Gaston to their tent the night before, looked just as snotty as he told the sergeant, "Your wife must stay behind precisely because she is your wife, God damn you both! As a military dependent she is carried on the official records as such, sergeant. El Generale's orders are that no official records shall ever show that anyone connected with his command went with those foreign thugs he hired off the record!"

The lieutenant spotted Captain Gringo and Gaston about then and added, with a nod, "Good morning. We were just talking about you."

Before either of them could answer, the sergeant demanded, with a puzzled scowl, "What am I, then, an *orphan?* I mean no disrespect, lieutenant, but, I have been regular army longer than any cabrón within sound of my voice right now!"

The officer shrugged and said, "That may be true. But I still outrank you and I still say you're coming with us for to cook for me. You are an army cook and I prefer army food to the beans and rice El Generale has issued those peon porters and their mujers. I am taking along my own rations. I need someone for to cook them. If you are captured, the books will say you were a deserter. If your wife was captured, the paperwork would smell of fish, since it's well known that army wives do not desert too often.''

The sergeant started to say something else. But the young officer snapped, ''I am through discussing the matter, Sergeant Morales. You have your orders. Get your gear together and be ready to move out in half an hour. Oh, I almost forgot. We are moving out disguised as civilians. Find yourself some nondescript clothing and a campesino hat. You can wear your boots, and ponchos are optional.''

Not giving the sergeant time to reply, the lieutenant turned to Captain Gringo and Gaston and said, ''You two, come with me. Our peones are assembled along with our gear, down this way.''

As they followed the snooty lieutenant, the sergeant was heard to announce to the world in general, ''All right, you cabrónes, a good soldado does as he is commanded. But remember, I am coming back, and he who touches my woman dies!''

As the soldiers of fortune followed the officer out of earshot, Gaston observed, ''Eh bien, I admire your sense of strategy, Lieutenant. If the surly enlisted man's wife remains here as a hostage to his good behavior, he shall no doubt behave très good, non?''

The officer permitted himself a frosty smile and replied, ''They are like children. One has to direct their minds in wholesome channels. As a matter of fact, Sergeant Morales was stretching the truth with that remark about his long military service. It is true he's been a soldado a long time. But up until a year or so ago he was cooking for the Granada forces.''

Captain Gringo frowned and asked, ''Can we trust him? How did he make sergeant for you guys if he started with the other side?''

''Easy. Morales is a very good cook. El Generale only shoots POWs who are of no use to anybody.''

Captain Gringo shrugged and said, ''Well, I guess you

guys know what you're doing." But he only said it to be polite. Had it been up to him, they wouldn't be taking along anybody just to serve the spoiled and pouty young officer. But if wasn't up to him, and what the hell, Morales probably wouldn't poison anyone if he really wanted to see his wife again someday.

Gaston asked if any other regulars were going along with them. The lieutenant shook his head and said El Generale had only assigned him to tag along and make sure the mission went according to plan. He said his name was Vallejo and that he wanted to be called Lieutenant Vallejo even out of uniform. Captain Gringo said that was jake with him, as long as everyone remembered to call him Captain. Vallejo didn't seem to think that was amusing.

At the end of the tent line, a ragged-ass band of mestizo men and women stood as patient as burros around a big mound of canvas-wrapped bales. Captain Gringo counted bales and noses and it came out one hell of a load for the dozen men and eight women. Vallejo indicated a loglike object under a tarp and said, "That is your machine gun. The ammo belts are in the pack under it. Now, if you will excuse me, señores, I must go get dressed for the costume party."

He marched off in step with himself as Captain Gringo and Gaston moved over to the people around the pile. The tall American smiled and said, "Buenos días, señores y señoras. Who is encargado here?"

The peones looked bewildered. Then an older man took off his sombrero and said softly, "Por favor, nobody is in charge here, señor. None of *us*, at any rate. El Generale said all of us had to do just what you officers said for to do, or he will burn our village."

Captain Gringo nodded understandingly and said, "Well, generals are like that. All right, my name is Ricardo Walker and I am called Captain Gringo for obvious reasons. This is Lieutenant Gaston Verrier, and if he tells anyone to do anything he'll have my backing, whether I'm in sight or not. How are you called, viejo?"

The old peon said, "I am called Nogales, Captain Gringo. My real name is Pedro, but everyone calls me Nogales for some reason and..."

"Nogales it is," Captain Gringo cut in, adding, "You'll be in charge of the civilians attached to this expedition. Can you do it?"

Nogales nodded hesitantly. A younger, bigger peon, who had been sulking in the rear of the class until now, protested, "For why are you putting Nogales over us, Captain Gringo? He is old and stupid!"

"How are you called, muchacho?"

"I am called Bruno. I am the toughest cabrón in our village too!"

"You look tough, Bruno. But when I asked who was in charge, nobody answered but Nogales here. So, tough shit. Do you want to fight, Bruno?"

The village bully blanched and stepped back a pace. Captain Gringo nodded curtly and said, "Bueno. Nogales, have you and your people eaten yet this morning?"

The old man shook his head sadly and replied, "We have been waiting here all night for our orders, Captain Gringo."

"All right. Look through the packs for some rations you can eat cold. We'll stop for a decent meal once we're clear of this unfriendly neighborhood. So don't overdo it."

As the old man smiled and began to open canvas flaps, Captain Gringo removed the tarp from the machine gun and handed it to Gaston. The weapon was a Maxim. So far so good. He opened the action and cursed. Gaston snorted in mutual disgust and said, "I could have told you. But look on the bright side. If it's still stuffed with petroleum jelly, none of these fumble-fingered rectal openings have had a chance to fuck up the action since it left the factory in this très greasy condition, non?"

Captain Gringo snapped the breech closed and muttered, "I'll have to field strip it total and adjust the head spacing before we dare to fire one round. Oh well, I didn't bring any heavy reading anyway, and we figure to be on the trail a few nights before we run into anything important enough to use it on.''

"True. I have always wanted to machine gun those damned bugs one meets in the jungle, but the little bastards won't hold still long enough.''

As they covered the Maxim, the cook, Morales, came to join them, wearing a big floppy sombrero and poncho. He spotted old Nogales handing out hardtack and roared, "What are you lousy mestizos doing in my rations? By the tits of the Virgin, I mean to flay your brown asses for this!''

Captain Gringo said, "Take it easy, sergeant. I told them to chow down.''

"*You* told them?'' Morales roared, adding, "Who in the fuck do you think you are? I, Morales, am in charge of the rations, damn your Anglo eyes!''

Captain Gringo said, "Oh, shit,'' and decked Morales with a left-handed sucker punch.

Morales was more surprised than hurt to find himself on his ass with blood running down his chin from a split lip. He rose to one knee, growled deep in his throat, and reached for something hanging at his side under his poncho. Then he froze as he found the muzzle of the tall American's .38 staring him down. Captain Gringo said calmly, "Go ahead and try it, sergeant. I don't give a shit either way. You're not sassing a green junior officer now.''

"You . . . you struck me!''

"No shit? I thought you just wanted to play stoop tag, Morales. Let go that pistol and stand at attention when you address an officer, damm it! I'm not going to hit you again. I promise you that the next time you give me any lip, I'll kill you.''

Morales moved his hands out from under the poncho as he rose, saluted, and hit a brace. Captain Gringo put his .38 away, returned the salute, and said, "At ease Sergeant. The hombre I have distributing the breakfast rations is called Nogales. You tell him what you want him to do with your rations packs and he'll do it. Carry on, Sergeant.''

He deliberately turned his back on the red-faced and bewildered noncom, partly to test him, as he knew Gaston was covering the son of a bitch in Gaston's usual sneaky way, and partly because he had had better things to worry about. He called Bruno over and said, "As soon as you finish that hardtack, we'll see about letting you pack the machine gun for me. We'll leave the tripod here, and I don't see any reason for the water jacket to be filled while were lugging it, so . . ."

"Can't my mujer pack the machine gun for you, Captain Gringo? My mujer is very strong and I have an old back injury."

"Right. We'll leave the water jacket filled. Water weighs eight pounds a gallon and the exercise will do you good. I have more gear here than all of us put together can carry So what's it going to be, Bruno? Do you want to sit down with a split lip too?"

"No, thank you, Captain Gringo. I was only trying to be helpful. My mujer is most surefooted and never drops anything I tell her to carry."

"Breno. I don't want her dropping *her* pack, either. If you drop the machine gun I'll blow your head off, and we wouldn't want that to happen, would we?"

Breno was saved from having to answer by the arrival of Lieutenant Vallejo, at last. He was dressed like a very rich peón under a flashy poncho and a flat crowned Spanish hat with fly tassels hanging from the stiff black brim. Captain Gringo resisted the impulse to suggest a rose between the lieutenant's teeth. The jerk-off carried a brace of six-guns under the poncho, and El Generale would probably be a pain if they left him behind, dead or alive.

Captain Gringo nodded at Vallejo and said, "We'll be moving out in a minute. Just wanted to put something in their guts for breakfast first."

"For why?" Vallejo asked in apparently sincere bewilderment.

Captain Gringo said, "Don't worry about it. I've tried to get people to work for me by just winding them up. But I can't seem to find any keys on their backs. Before we get in any more trouble, could we settle on some ground rules, Lieutenant? As I get the picture, the general's sending you along as an observer. With me in command, right?''

Vallejo shrugged and replied, ''My orders are not specific on that. I suppose as long as I think you're doing your job right, I won't have to issue you any orders. Why?''

''Just wanted to get it straight. I, ah, had to hang a left on your cook, Sergeant Morales, just now. I think we got his position in the pecking order straightened out. Any objections?''

Vallejo smiled for the first time since they'd met, albeit coldly, and said, ''Be my guest. I would wave done so earlier, if gentlemen fought with their fists. I don't have to tell you what will happen if you ever lay a finger on *me* without my permission, do I?''

''No. I said I liked to see all the cards on the table, and if you don't cross me I won't cross you. Shall we get the show on the road?''

''By all means, Captain Gringo. I am looking forward to seeing how a famous military expert does things. I shall just, how you say, watch?''

Captain Gringo nodded curtly and muttered in English, ''Watch this, then, Shavetail!'' as he turned and called out, ''Gaston! Front and center! Bring Nogales with you on the double!''

Gaston dragged the confused peon over and asked, ''What's up, Dick?''

''We're moving out. I'll take the point. You bring up the rear. Nogales, you and your people will load up and walk in single file between us.''

''Por favor, señor, who carries what and . . .''

''*You* were put in charge of that, old man. So *do* it!'' snapped Captain Gringo as he strode over to the pile the machine gun sat atop, calling out, ''Bruno! Get your fat ass here on the double!''

As the big peon joined him, the tall American had already opened the petcock on the Maxim's water jacket and was removing it from its tripod as the water dribbled like piss. He handed it to Bruno, saying, "Here, let this drain, since you've been such a good boy. Then wrap it in that tarp and hoist it to your shoulder. Grab that ammo with your free hand and catch up with me poco tiempo. I'll be at the head of the column, and you'll be right at my heels if you know what's good for you."

Captain Gringo looked around, saw everyone busy as bees, and started walking, not looking back. He spotted the hard rubber hilt of a machete sticking out of a loose bundle and grabbed it on the fly, even though there was nothing important growing in his way as he entered the palmetto scrub. He'd need some guidance once they were out a way, but meanwhile the sun through the overcast threw enough shadows to show which way was west, at least. He wanted to shake out the kinks and rub in his dominance a bit more before he admitted that even he needed occasional advice, when and if he asked for it.

He heard trotting footsteps behind him. He just kept walking at a brisk, but not too brisk, pace until Lieutenant Vallejo fell in at his side to say, in wonder, "I can't believe it. They're all lined up behind you and somehow everyone seems to be packing his or her fair share with no further orders from you or Verrier!"

Captain Gringo shrugged and said, "It's a trick I learned from General Grant. Not Grant himself, of course. They told the story at West Point. Once upon a time General Grant needed a new aide-de-camp. There were three new shavetails fresh from the Point who wanted the job. Old Grant called the first one in and said, 'Mister, if I told you I wanted a fifty-foot flagstaff erected in front of my tent, how would you go about it?' How would *you* go about it, Lieutenant Vallejo?"

Vallejo shrugged and said, "I suppose I would gather a work detail, go out in the forest for to find a proper tree, and . . ."

"Send in the next applicant," Captain Gringo cut in, explaining, "That's what the first shavetail told Grant he'd do. The second one said he'd fill out the proper work orders and vouchers for the engineer corps. So Grant sent him away, too. The third guy got the job. His answer was that if the general wanted a fucking flagstaff he'd step out of the tent, grab the first passing noncom, and tell him the general wanted a fucking flagstaff, in one fucking hour, period!''

Vallejo had to think about that awhile before he got it. He shook his head and asked, ''Is that how you got things done in the U.S. Army?''

''It's the way *I* did. We had some assholes, too. That's the main reason I'm down here soldiering the hard way. I led a troop of the Tenth Cav against Apache for a while. It was a black outfit. White officers, of course. Most of us learned pretty quick that life's too short to stand over a man and give him detailed instructions to brush his teeth and wipe his ass. Tell the average soldier to move around to the left and you don't really have to tell him to keep his head down and shoot the Apache first, see?''

''Ah, but those pobrecitos following us are not trained soldados.''

''So what? It takes a military genius to pick up a pack and carry it?''

He stopped and turned around, adding, ''Speaking of military geniuses, where's that fucking Bruno with my Maxim and ammo?''

The ragged column in their wake staggered to a confused halt as they saw him stop. That gave the short bandy-legged girl packing the Maxim, ammo, and backpack of rations time to gain on the head of the column. She was breathing sort of funny as she staggered up to them and gasped, ''Forgive me, Captain Gringo, but you walk so fast!''

''Give me that machine gun and sit on the ammo a minute, muchacha. Who the hell are you, and where the hell is Bruno?''

She sank down gratefully and gasped, ''I am called Florita, señor. Bruno told me to carry for him because of his bad back.''

''Nogales!'' Captain Gringo roared.

The old man dropped the pack he'd been carrying on his head and ran forward, removing said hat as Captain Gringo demanded, "Where's that good-for-nothing Bruno?"

Nogales answered, "Por favor, I do not know, Captain Gringo. He said something about a bad back as I passed him last."

Captain Gringo whistled between his teeth. Gaston whistled back and dog-trotted up to the head of the column. Gaston took in the scene at a glance and said, "Eh bien, we are discussing young men who complain of fatigued spines, no doubt?"

"Yeah, the prick loaded his mujer, here, with both their loads. He didn't fall back past you, did he?"

Gaston smiled thinly and said, "He tried to."

Captain Gringo said, "Oh. All right, everybody, let's move it out as before. Florita, stay close with that ammo. I'll pack the Maxim for now."

He started walking west, allowing them to think for themselves, but not too much, as they fell into place behind him once more.

Lieutenant Vallejo also thought for himself as they made the first hundred yards or so in silence. Then he asked softly, "Did Verrier do what I think he might have done, captain?"

Captain Gringo shook his head and said, "There's no *might* about it. When Gaston's bringing up the rear, it's not a good idea to straggle."

"I did not hear a shot."

Captain Gringo wasn't sure he wanted the snooty lieutenant to know about the knife Gaston wore under his collar at the nape of his neck, so he just said, "What can I tell you? You know what they say about Frenchmen fucking with their mouth and fighting with their feet."

"Is he that good? With his feet, I mean? He's not very big, and he's rather elderly, no?"

"Bruno might have been counting on that. Forget it. We're still close enough to camp for someone to smell him in a few hours. Let *them* worry about it."

Vallejo shrugged and said, "Nobody but the ants will worry about him now. El Generale is marching up the coast this morning to deal with other problems to the north.

"Yeah? Let's not tell your cook, then. I don't want to lose any more help until we eat these supplies a little lighter."

Vallejo said, "He already knows. Why did you think he was acting so crazy? His mujer is most attractive and a bit of a flirt. But he knows as long as he behaves, he may someday hope to see her again."

They walked on a way before Vallejo mused, "I hope *she* behaves. Buckets of blood will flow if our burly sergeant ever hears of her having anything to do with another hombre. He only married his Dulcenita a short while ago and . . ."

"Kee-rist!" Captain Gringo cut in. "Is Morales the *husband* of that little Dulcenita?"

Vallejo shot him a puzzled look, then brightened and said, "Oh, that's right, you *do* know Dulcenita. She was one of the girls I sent to your tent with refreshments last night. Did they take care of you all right?"

Less than five miles from the army camp they ran out of palmetto scrub and into a swamp. A big one, studded with cypress knees and covered with a green scum that smelled like frog shit. Captain Gringo turned to Lieutenant Vallejo and asked, "Which way, north or south?"

The young officer answered, "Don't ask me. I'm only an observer for El Generale."

The tall American turned and saw that his people were bunching up, and while he didn't approve of that, this wasn't the time and place for basic training. So he called out, "All right, which one of you knows the best way around this swamp?"

No answer.

Gaston came over to join him and the lieutenant, musing softly, "Me and my big knife. I was just discussing the late

Bruno with the peones at my end of the column. Aside from being a shirker, he was a local nimrod who hunted in the backwaters for frog legs, Spanish moss, and other things he could carry without straining his poor aching back. I fear *he* was supposed to be the guide El Generale mentioned, non?''

Captain Gringo shrugged and said, "Forget it. He didn't figure to guide us worth a shit once he deserted." He took out his ordnance map and spread it on the sand as the three squatted for a look at it. The swamp that blocked further easy passage west wasn't on the map. The cartographers had just put lots of marsh-grass symbols all up and down the Mosquito Coast and you were supposed to work out the details for yourself.

Captain Gringo said, "If we follow the sandy cuesta north, we hit the British trade route and maybe the British. It's out of our way, anyway. Okay, we trend south-southwest and see what happens. If there's any old way across to the higher ground on the far side, some Indian will have noticed and blazed a trail. Let's go."

Vallejo rose, along with the two soldiers of fortune, but protested, "It is getting hot. When are we going to stop for la siesta?"

Captain Gringo glanced up at the sky and said, "When it's even hotter. It's nowhere's near noon yet, lieutenant. With luck it ought to be raining fire and salt in a little while, anyhow."

He called out to his lower-ranking followers and pointed southwest with his machete, announcing, "Vamanos, muchachas y muchachos!" and started to turn away. Then he saw that little Florita was having trouble getting to her feet with the heavy pack and ammo. So he hauled her up, saying, "I'm sorry I can't carry the ammo, too. But I need one hand free with this machete."

"I shall do my best, señor," she replied, trying not to cry. He looked at Vallejo, who wasn't packing anything but his six-guns and silly hat, and said, "Lietenant, you'd better carry the ammo. This girl's pack must weigh sixty pounds or more."

Vallejo took out a skinny cheroot and lit it, saying, "I came along as an observer, not as a porter. Do I look like a peon to you?"

"I'd tell you what you look like to me, but there's a lady present. Good grief, what in the hell are you smoking, lieutenant? It smells like fucking *violets!*"

Vallejo blew a perfumed cloud his way and replied, "As a matter of fact, there are violet petals mixed with the tobacco. They're made in Cuba for discriminating customers."

"Okay, so you buy your smokes from a whorehouse and we've still gotta carry that ammo. Be a sport, lieutenant. You'll still have one hand free to jerk off under your poncho, and whatever this little dame is, she ain't a burro."

He'd deliberately phrased it so it looked like Vallejo had a choice. The prissy officer shrugged and said, "Oh, very well," and relieved the peon girl of the ammo as Captain Gringo turned away and started trudging through the scrub with the Maxim on one shoulder and the machete handy to take care of anything else slowing him down.

Vallejo had been right about it getting hotter. Despite the overcast, or perhaps because of it, by late morning they were staggering through a steamroom a lot of sweaty frogs and alligators had obviously used first. They were making lousy time. But Captain Gringo knew that if he pushed his people any harder on the first day out they'd start falling apart by the second. El Generale Portola had recruited too few locals for the heavy loads he'd issued, and, despite all that bullshit about them being swamp-running Indians, they were simply agricultural peones, used to the pace of life visitors to the tropics discounted as lazy. Captain Gringo had been down here long enough to know that Latin Americans worked as hard as anyone could in this climate, if they expected to make it to forty. The perpetual heat offered three crops a year if a campasino rolled with the punches and didn't try to reap more than a Pennsylvania Dutchman's one good harvest from his three tropic plantings. While ever warm, the local weather tended to give too much or too little water from month to month, and the weeds were maniacal. So the "lazy" campassino actually put in more work with his hoe and spade in a year than the average Anglo farmer, if you added it all up. The secret lay in spreading out the work. The twelve-hour work day a Yankee boss expected would kill anyone who tried it down here. The Ladino peon worked an hour or so at a time, then took a break. That "lazy" guy leaning against a wall with his sombrero pulled down over his face figured to get up again in a while and go back to work. In the sticky heat, sleep was taken in small doses, too. Unlike people to the north, Ladinos broke the day into two-or three-hour fragments of work, rest, play, or whatever. Hence, the reason visitors were bemused to find a Ladino asleep at noon or plowing a field at midnight.

Captain Gringo moved between two clumps of sea grape and found himself atop a sandy rise surrounded by sea grape, palmetto, and Spanish bayonet. He laid the tarp-wrapped Maxim on the warm sand, stuck the machete in the ground beside it, and called out, "Trail break. Nogales, front and center!"

The old man staggered up to him, under his own load, and Captain Gringo said, "We'll be here a while. It's about to start raining again. Hard, judging by the way the wind's picking up and blowing against the trades. I don't want anyone chilled. Have your people build lean-tos and start a small Indian fire in front of each. I know it sounds silly right now. But you'll never get a bed of rain-resistant coals started unless you start with dry fuel."

The old man dropped his load and got to it. Captain Gringo saw that the girl, Florita, had dropped herself as well as her load to the warm sand and was staring down at it like she was about to puke. He said, "Take off that pack and move over to that palmetto, Florita. Don't drink any water just yet."

As she moved to obey, Lieutenant Vallejo shot them a curious look. The tall American said, "Heat stroke, I think. Told you she wasn't a burro. Where's your cook? I want him to break out some rations and grub the troops."

"Sergeant Morales is my personal cook, if you don't mind, Captain."

"I do mind. He can cook for you. He can bend over for you. But he's going to put some strong hot coffee in the rest of the outfit if we're going to get any fucking where this year. I'm making you mess officer. Before you say anything dumb, lieutenant, I'm not *asking* you. I'm *telling* you! You can still catch up with El Generale if you want to pick up your marbles and run home."

Vallejo's eyes narrowed. Then he shrugged and said, "I do not have to take orders from you, Yanqui. But since you *asked* if I wished for to act as mess officer, I shall give the required orders."

He removed his poncho, dropped it on the sand, and stomped off to do as he'd been told. Gaston joined Captain Gringo, saying, "I heard the last of that exchange, Dick. I don't think that schoolboy likes his teacher."

"Fuck what he likes. I don't care if anyone leaves an apple on my desk or not."

"Eh, bien, just make sure he doesn't present you with a stick of dynamite or a bullet in the derriere. We've both met officers like Vallejo before, and stupid men make me très nervous. One can work out deals with devils, but idiots are liable to do *anything*, even when it is not in their own best interests. Perhaps our perfumed wonder should have an, ah, accident?"

"Not until we cash that certified check. Hold the thought. I seem to have a sick girl on my hands."

He moved over to where Florita reclined in the dappled palmetto shade and hunkered down beside her. He took out a kerchief, wet it from his belt canteen, and removed her straw sombrero, saying, "Hold still. This ought to help."

As he wiped her beaded brow he saw, now that she didn't have her little heart-shaped face shaded, that Florita wasn't bad-looking. She was far from being a Gibson Girl. Despite the fact she couldn't have been twenty, hard work and lousy nutrition had put lines on her brown face that few Yankee women expected to see in their mirrors before thirty or so. She'd look even older by the time she had a few kids. He could see by the fullness of her thin cotton blouse that she hadn't nursed any yet. Her breasts were big, but firm, with perky little nipples showing through the perspiration-soaked cotton. He said, "You're sweating too much for heat stroke. You've already survived vomito negro, of course?"

"Sí; what the Anglos in Greytown call yellow jack swept through our village when I was very little. My brothers and sisters died, but I did not, and since then I have never had el vomito negro again."

"Hmm, it could be malaria. I have some quinine here. I buy it as regular as cigars and . . ."

"Por favor, I know what is wrong with me, Señor Deek," she cut in, blushing slightly as she said, "I ate too many palmetto berries. I have been picking them as we walked down the cuesta and . . ."

"Hold it, Florita," he said with a puzzled frown, adding, "Nobody eats palmetto berries. They're *poisonous*, right?"

"They make one sick to one's stomach if one eats too many." She nodded.

So he asked, "Why in the hell did you eat them, then? Do you want to go back to your village that badly?"

She shook her head and said, "No, some brute like Bruno would only rape me again. Is it true Bruno is no more? Forgive me, I did not wish for to listen, but I could not help overhearing some of what you and the old Frenchman said."

He said, "You don't have to worry about Bruno anymore, Florita. But how come he mistreated you in the first place? Don't you have an alcalde in your village to protect pretty young muchachas?"

She shook her head and said, "No. Our village is no more than a cluster of huts, since los Anglos came to colonize this part of the world. They sent our padre and officials away. They said we were all subjects of their Queen Victoria now, but none of us speak English and . . ."

He stopped her by saying, "I know about Anglo-Saxon

colonial policy. I used to be an Anglo-Saxon. Let's get back
to poisoning ourselves with palmetto berries. Why did you do
it, Florita?''

She lowered her lashes and blushed beet red as she murmured,
''I wished for to be a passionate woman. The brujas say that
if one eats a few fruits of the saw palmetto, it acts like
Spanish fly Now. I am not sure they know what they are
talking about. I have eaten at least a handful, and all I feel is
very very seasick!''

''You look better now than you did before. If you can't
throw up, just sit tight and I'll get some black coffee down
you as soon as it's ready. That should set you free one way or
another. Meanwhile, why in the hell were you trying to dose
yourself with the local witchcraft aphrodisiac? Who are you
so hot for, Florita?''

She sighed and said, ''In God's truth, no one, Señor Deek.
I do not know what is wrong with me, but I am a frigid bitch.
That is what my husband called me when he left me for
another, and what Bruno used to call me before he beat me. I
thought perhaps if I ate palmetto berries, like the brujas
said . . .''

''Querida, you're talking loco en la cabeza,'' he cut in
gently, before adding, ''Bruno's not with us anymore. So
who in hell's about to call you a frigid anything? You've been
walking right behind me since we left El Generale and I don't
remember any of the others getting forward with you.''

She said, ''Sí. They all know you have chosen me for to be
your adelita on the trail.''

He blinked and muttered, ''Oh boy!'' before switching
back to Spanish to assure her, ''Don't worry, Florita. I hardly
ever rape little girls, and when I do, I never call them
names.''

''Don't you think I am pretty?''

''I think you're very pretty, and sort of confusing, too. You
just said you didn't enjoy sex with any man, Florita.''

''I don't. I have tried to, God knows. But nothing happens,
and after a time it gets most uncomfortable as you all shove

those silly things in and out of me. The brujas say it is just my nature to be as I am. They say some women were just never meant to enjoy it.''

He nodded understandingly and said, ''I don't know much about witchcraft, Florita, but our doctors say much the same, and since I'm neither a doctor nor a witch, let's not worry about it.''

''You will not be angry tonight when I do not respond to your lovemaking as a woman is supposed to?''

He laughed and said, ''I'm not going to get angry because I'm not even going to try, Florita.''

She started to cry. He started to ask her if she was nuts. Then he thought about the way guerrilla bands were usually set up and said, ''I see. You want to be head adelita, but you don't want to get laid. Bueno. I'm not about to post any bans on a palmetto tree, Florita, but stick close to me and let the others think what they wish. Stay here for now, though. I've got to see about food and shelter for everyone.''

He took off his canteen and left it with her as he rose to look around and see how the others had been doing while he was enjoying such a weird conversation. The machete-wielding peones had done pretty good, and just in time. A big fat gob of rain plopped down on the brim of Captain Gringo's hat as he stared in approval at the thatch lean-tos and blue smoke plumes spread across the rise. He turned and called the sick girl to heel before striding over to old Nogales, who stood by his wrapped Maxim and empty lean-to, obviously hoping for approval.

Captain Gringo did approve, and said so, as he saw his bedroll and personal gear already spread out under the thatch, with a little smudge fire close enough to the opening to refuel from the neat pile of palemtto stalks under the overhang without leaving the bedding. Nogales said the sullen cook, out of sight down the line, would soon be serving, and asked, ''Has Florita agreed to serve you, Captain Gringo, or do you wish for someone else to bring your food and coffee when it's ready?''

Captain Gringo said, "Florita's sick. She'll be sheltering here with me. Tell Morales to send two rations or bring it over himself, just so we get it."

The old man shot a knowing look at the little peon girl as Florita joined them. Captain Gringo told her, "Duck under there. If you have to vomit, try to miss the bedding. I'll be back in a minute."

He walked toward the center of camp as more gobs of rain plopped down at scattered intervals. Old Nogales said, "As you see, we built your lean-to facing discreetly away. We thought you might wish privacy during your siesta, no?"

Captain Gringo didn't answer. Anything he could have said would have sounded stupid. He saw Gaston and Lieutenant Vallejo standing near the larger cooking fire of Sergeant Morales, rank having its privileges when the noon mess figures to be served under a thunderstorm at any minute. The tall American asked Vallejo how many carbines they had in the packs for the others. Vallejo asked why the hell El Generale would have issued weapons for more porters. Captain Gringo growled, "Ask a stupid question and you get a stupid answer. Okay, you, me, Gaston, and Morales are the only armed men here. Morales is busy. I've got a sick friend to nurse. That leaves you two to stand the first watch. How do you want to work it, Gaston? Flip a coin?"

Vallejo blanched and said, "I do not stand guard. I am an *officer!*"

Before Captain Gringo could tell him what he really was, Gaston said, "Eh bien, I'd feel safer if a *man* was on duty. I'll take the first two hours, Dick."

Captain Gringo nodded and said, "I'll take the second. By then, if it's still raining, anybody creeping around in the jungle will have drowned. If it's stopped in four hours, we'll be moving on. So it evens out."

He had told Nogales he wanted his rations brought to him. But now that he was here, he picked up a couple of mess kits and told Morales to dish out his coffee and grub. Morales said he wasn't ready yet. Vallejo told him not to be an idiot. So the surly cook filled Captain Gringo's kits and the tall American headed back to Florita and his lean-to. He made it just in time. As he got under the thatch with her, the sky popped open like a bursting rubber and rain started coming down in sheets. The fire out front tried, but hissed out like a dying bucket of snakes as the light outside went dark as evening no matter what the clock said.

He saw that Florita was under the cotton flannel top sheet, which seemed a good idea. Then, as she reached for the mess kit and coffee cup he offered her, he saw that she wasn't wearing her blouse anymore. He noticed her ruffled peon skirts had been wadded into a pillow at the head of the bedroll, too. So he didn't ask if she was naked under the sheet. He just wondered why.

He sat cross-legged near the opening, eating and drinking with her, as distant thunder rumbled and the rain pattered on the thick thatch above them. It was a little chilly as well as almost dry under the overhang. He said, "Don't take this the wrong way, querida. But I'm getting under the covers with you. Pneumonia in the tropics feels silly as hell, so I try to avoid it."

He knew the best way to get a good chill in this tricky climate was to bundle up in wet duds, so he started taking his damp linen off as she sighed in resignation and said she understood.

He wasn't sure he did. It felt mighty comfy to slide under the flannel with a naked lady who'd already warmed the bedding with her own body heat. But when he automatically started to reach for her, he remembered her female complaint and abstained. Sort of. It was impossible to share the bedroll without their naked flesh touching here and there under the covers. He fished out a cigar and matches and lit up. It felt sort of dumb smoking on his stomach, but what else was a man with a dawning erection to do if he didn't want to look like a tent pole next to an unwilling bed partner?

He asked if she wanted to smoke. She said she didn't, explaining that while she was getting over the effects of the palmetto berries, even the idea of smoking anything made her retch. He said he was sorry and put out his cigar. It was a dumb position to smoke in, anyway. She said he was muy simpatico and added, "I think the brujas may have been right about saw-palmetto fruit, after all. I am starting to feel, ah, odd."

"Oh? You mean sexy?"

"I don't know. Maybe I am just so dizzy I just don't care. Usually, when I know a man is about to stick his old thing in me, it makes me feel like I am about to vomit. But since I have been feeling like I was about to vomit all this time, with nobody sticking anything in me . . ."

He laughed and said, "You sure have a romantic way with words. Try and get some sleep. We won't be here long, and once this rain lets up I'll be pushing you all to make up for lost time."

She started to cry again. He propped himself up on one elbow, frowned down at her, and asked, "*Now* what in the hell is the matter?"

"You think I am ugly. I was afraid you would think I was ugly. Nobody finds me desirable as a woman. It is all so unfair!"

He started to tell her she was nuts. But they'd already established that, and, what the hell, it wasn't as if she were a blushing virgin. She just had something wrong with her plumbing, or maybe with her little brain. It wasn't his problem. He had all the problems he needed.

One of them, at the moment, seemed to be a raging erection. He muttered, "Jesus, I'm sexually confused, too. This is really nuts."

"Have I done something to make you angry, Señor Deek?"

"No, I'm angry at this idiotic appendage down here with a mind of its own. If you were a frothing-at-the-mouth sex fiend it would probably go soft on me. I've tried talking sense to the damned thing, but does it ever listen?"

She said, "You may abuse me with it, if you must."

He snorted in disgust and said, "No, thanks. My dong may

be an animal, but *I'm* not. Go to sleep, Florita. Talking about it isn't about to calm anybody down.''

"Can you go to sleep, with your desires for sex aroused?"

"No. I'm going to clean my machine gun. I've been meaning to, anyway, and if there's one thing a dirty machine gun is, it ain't sexy."

He sat up, hauled the wrapped Maxim in its tarp between them, and unwrapped it. Florita watched him fieldstrip it, but as she had no idea how anything more complicated than a hand tool worked, her eyes grew heavy-lidded, and by the time he'd wiped most of the steel reasonably clean and reassembled it, she lay on her side asleep with her bare back to him. He opened the ammo pack, took out a belt of .30-30, armed the Maxim, then put it on safe and placed it atop the folded tarp at the foot of the bedroll. He looked at his pocket watch before he lay back down beside the naked girl. Gaston would be coming for him soon, and he hadn't come at all, but what the hell, the distraction had gotten rid of his erection, until he thought about it.

Florita's knees were drawn up as she lay on her side with her brown rump vulnerable to perhaps a sneaky entrance if he lay on his side, sort of moved down, and . . . "Forget it," he told himself. "If the dame's too goosey to do it with her own husband, awake, she'd come up fighting for sure if she woke up with a strange dong in her!"

He didn't want to disturb her by smoking. He'd feel silly as hell if she woke up to catch him jerking off. So he just lay there making like a tent pole as he listened to the rain and waited for Gaston. The rain was easing up a bit. Somewhere a bird or howler monkey was making weirder than usual noises and . . . that was a human voice he was listening to!

As he sat up, groping on his pants and boots, he heard the report of Gaston's .38, well to the south. He grabbed the Maxim and rose with it, the belt trailing on the sand behind him as he ran east into the dripping brush. Other voices were shouting in confusion and someone was talking back to Gaston's .38 with a .30-30. Captain Gringo pictured the layout of their improvised camp as he circled well around it through cover, keeping track of Gaston's occasional .38 reports. Where the hell were Morales and Vallejo with those .45s?

He spotted something broom-straw yellow, moving in the scrub ahead and circled wider. He knew Gaston was firing from cover at the south edge of their camp. He knew where the camp was and had the range on that one straw sombrero he'd spotted. So it was simple enough to work around to the flank of the guys giving Gaston a hard time for some reason. He snapped off the safety switch on the Maxim and eased forward, the heavy but empty jacketed machine gun braced on his hip with the muzzle trained the way he was looking. So when he spotted the guys Gaston was holding at pistol range south of their camp, all he had to do was pull the trigger. The Maxim bellowed like a cross between a woodpecker and an angry bull. Sombreros, palmetto fronds, and what looked like tossed bloody salad filled the air as he dug in his heels and traversed the Maxim back and forth across the band's right flank.

He couldn't see how many there were or how many he was really hitting and not just scaring out of a year's growth. But whoever they were, they wanted no further part of these parts and started moving back poco tiempo, which was an awful mistake on their part. Because Captain Gringo still had half the belt left when they broke cover.

In the end, some of them must have gotten away, because when Gaston moved out to join Captain Gringo over the chopped-up bodies in the chopped-up scrub, they counted fourteen hats and thirteen Krag rifles to go with only a dozen bodies. Gaston said, "It's about *time* you got here!"

"I overslept. Who do you figure these guys used to be?"

Gaston finished reloading, put his .38 away, and said, "Ladrónes, from their costume. Guerrillas, from those new rifles. Whoever they were, they were not well trained. I heard them shouting back and forth like schoolchildren as they advanced up the cuesta. I don't think they knew we were here. When I called a challenge, they responded in a most rude manner. The rest you know.''

Captain Gringo hefted the Maxim to one shoulder as he grunted, ''Not quite. I circled the whole camp and the only fire I heard from our side was that little peashooter of yours Gaston. Where the hell were Vallejo and Morales while all this was going on?''

''Merde alors, how should I know? I was aiming the other way. Fortunately, none of those idiots knew I was only shooting in the air from good cover as I moved about to sound like a small army. I knew that sooner or later my adoring child would come to his proud papa's assistance with that more serious weapon.''

''Don't explain guerrilla tactics, damm it. Explain where Vallejo and . . . never mind, here come the assholes now.''

The mufti-clad officer and his cook were frog-marching one of the peon porters ahead of them with drawn pistols. Some of the other men from camp were trailing at a cautious distance. Vallejo called out, ''This man was trying to run away. I caught him north of camp.''

Captain Gringo smiled pleasantly and said, ''Right. You were running that way to secure our lines of communication. Morales, what's *your* story?''

The surly cook shrugged and said, ''I have no story. When an old soldier hears shooting he hits the dirt and stays there until someone tells him what to do.''

Captain Gringo nodded, turned to the frightened peon Vallejo had the drop on, and asked, ''How are you called, muchacho?''

''Por favor, Captain Gringo, I am called Ernesto, and I am very sorry I lost my head and ran.''

''Not as sorry as you'll be if you ever do it again. Take this machine gun and don't go anyplace with it while we police up the area. Nogales! Front and center!''

As the old man gingerly came forward, Lieutenant Vallejo spotted a body in the chopped-up shrubbery ahead and asked, ''My God, how many of them did we get?''

Captain Gringo let the "we" pass and replied, "Not as many as we tried to. At least a couple got away. I don't see packs or adelitas. So these guys were a forward patrol of whatever." He turned to Nogales and said, "I want you and these guys to gather guns, ammo, and anything else of interest you find on those bodies. But make it fast. We're moving out in five minutes."

He headed back for the main camp, calling out, "All right, everybody up? Drop your cocks and grab your socks. La siesta is over for sure!"

The swamp water came to their waists to chill their balls as the afternoon heat steamed their brains and filled their eyes with muggy mist and humming insects. Captain Gringo had already explained why he'd ordered his people due west across the swamplands instead of farther south to look for a dry crossing, but as the muck sucked at his boots, Lieutenant Vallejo pestered him once more about the route he'd chosen, saying, "This is madness, captain. We should have searched for a ford to the north if, as you suggest, those guerrillas were waiting for us to the south."

Captain Gringo growled, "I wasn't suggesting it. I was saying it. The rifles and ammo we salvaged from that combat patrol are spanking new, and they had too much pocket change for a band of mere ladrónes. They were well-funded irregulars. Probably fighting for Granada. They were headed for the last known address of your general, and they opened up on Gaston when they heard a challenge from Portola's direction."

He stumbled over a submerged root, fought to keep from going under with the reloaded Maxim he packed on his shoulder, and added, "Forget 'em. They can't dog our footsteps if we don't leave footsteps for 'em to dog. The map says there's nothing much but blank paper the way we're headed. Ain't it fun to play explorer?"

"You're going to get us lost in the jungle, damm it!"

"I sure hope so. If nobody knows where we are, nobody can shoot us. It's going to take Gaston at least a couple of days to teach our porters and at least a couple of tough adelitas basic rifle drill. I don't want to meet anyone important before our guys know which end of a Krag the bullet comes out of, do you?"

Vallejo sniffed and said, "You know what I think of arming peones. Up until now, our only hold on them has been that we have guns and they have not. What if they turn on us?"

"We'll be in a hell of a mess. So will they, unless they know how to read maps and don't think El Generale was serious about burning their village if they screwed up. I'm more worried about double-crosses from higher up than lower down, lieutenant. I know why Morales was considered expendable. Why do you suppose Portola figured he could spare *you?*"

Vallejo gasped in surprise, waded on, and snapped, "Don't be ridiculous! I was El Generale's most valuable aide-de-camp. He said he was depending on me to see that you two, ah, outside consultants carried out this most important mission properly."

Captain Gringo hacked a hanging mossy vine out of their way with the machete in his free hand before he grunted, "Yeah, that's why he sent us out with unarmed peones and no guides. The map he issued us is a peach, too. It's scaled way too large for cross-country work, with only the gross features of a mighty complicated terrain. How do you get to be an aide-de-camp in the León forces, lieutenant? Do you send in a box top with fifty words or less about how much you admire the junta in León, or what?"

"My uncle happens to be a *member* of the ruling junta in León!" the junior officer answered smugly. Captain Gringo nodded and muttered, "Out of the mouths of babes. Okay, we're toilet paper, like I figured. The question now is whether we've been flushed and forgotten or whether El Generale really means to burn our little guys out if we fuck up and bring 'em back alive."

Vallejo said he had no idea what the tall American was talking about. So Captain Gringo stopped talking. The light was getting really lousy and the water they were wading through was haunted by critters that hunted mostly in the dark. He twanged through some glandular celery-looking growth that smelled like rubber cement when the machete bit into it, and, when he stepped through the gap, he found the water shallower and loused up with even more tangled vegetation. He said, "We're coming to a hammock. What time is it, lieutenant?"

Vallejo consulted his pocket watch and said, "A little after five. Why?"

"The 'gators are most dangerous just after sundown, and sundown comes at six pretty regular, in this neck of the tropics. I think we've found as good a place to dig in for the night as we're about to before someone loses a leg."

It wasn't that easy. As always, in the jungle, the vegetation grew wildest where there was an edge to compete for. Evolution had gone nuts around the skirts of the dry land encircled by blackwater swamp. Stuff that grew best with wet roots wrestled with stuff that grew best dry but was willing to test the pool with its toes. The machete twanged through solid springy wood as well as mushy pulp, and Captain Gringo was dripping with sweat as well as swampwater by the time he hacked through to dry land, if you wanted to call it that. The ground between the tall timber growing on the hammock was covered with what looked and smelled like rotting banana peels, mossy fallen branches, and a collection of mushrooms that would have confused a botanist considerably.

Captain Gringo braced the Maxim over a fallen log, stuck the point of his machete in said log, and then sat on it, wearily, as he watched the others file through the gap onto more or less dry land. He spotted old Nogales, called him over, and said, "We're camping here. Fires first, to dry everyone out before sunset turns the tap to cold. Make sure you scrape the forest duff away before building the fires. I don't like surprises, and that shit can smolder pretty good under the surface, once it warms up some.''

Nogales looked injured and said he'd been building fires on the surface of Nicaragua for some time. He said to leave everything to him. That was the trouble with giving a peon a gun and other authority. Captain Gringo just nodded and said, ''Bueno.'' With luck, nobody would start to plot against him before they won a few firefights with those Krags and started feeling more important.

Vallejo wandered off to take a leak, smoke a violet cheroot, or something. Little Florita joined him on the log and snuggled close, to warm her chilled hips, to show off for the other mujeres, or both. He absentmindedly put an arm around her waist. It felt better than resting his bare palm on the somewhat gluggy log.

Gaston was last through the gap, of course. The Frenchman now had a rifle slung as well as his pack on his back. He unloaded and sat down on the far side of Florita with a sigh. He said, ''Eh bien. Let's claim this place as a private republic and just stay here. I have been thinking as you led us through that evil-smelling puddle, Dick. I know it's a nasty habit, but I was thinking anyway. Has it occurred to you this whole très ridicule expedition is a feint?''

In English, Captain Gringo replied, ''What was your first clue? Portola knew Granadine guerrillas were just south of him. He wouldn't have issued us this Maxim if he wanted them to kill us for sure. But he would have sent us with some decent fighting men and materiel if he was really concerned about our health. I just found out how Vallejo got his so-called commission. It was a political favor. Portola had longer than us to find out that the jerk-off was useless, and it only took us a day.''

''Eh bien, the only question before the house is what are we to do now. I don't think Portola gives a fart at the moon about that dam and his damned Indians. I find it très difficult to work up even that much concern. On the other hand, the dam site is right on the Costa Rican border, non?''

Captain Gringo patted Florita's wet rump and told her to take the machete and build them a nice little house of twigs before it started to rain again. As she scampered off, waving the machete proudly, Captain Gringo said, "Never discuss strategy in front of anyone, even in English. You never know how much of the drift may be getting through."

"True. I once managed to anticipate a droll incident in a North African alley that way, and I *still* don't know enough Arabic to matter. But, now that we are free to plot in any language, and all shit of the bull aside, the certified check I carry next to my heart is probably going to bounce whether its wrapped in rubber or not. If we forgot the carrot on the stick and just scampered on to Costa Rica, we would be no worse off than we were before we met all these sneaky people, non?"

"What about our campasinos?"

Gaston shrugged and asked, "Did either of us give birth to them? The poor bastards will suffer either way. El Generale may not be about to follow through on his threat to their home village. If he sent us this way to make noise and attract attention, he doubtless has plans to march his army somewhere else as we distract the Granadines with machine-gun fire, non?"

Captain Gringo nodded and said, "Yeah, that works. It explains why he'd see fit to issue us a Maxim and plenty of ammo without handing out one lousy rifle."

"Eh bien, he knew your reputation for sounding like a whole army on occasion. As I said, this expedition is merely a feint. Portola's not expecting us even to make it to that dam site. Merde alors, for all we know, he could be in league with that British construction company. How much would it take to bribe anyone on either side here?"

Captain Gringo smiled thinly and said, "Not much. But aren't you sort of curious about the third or fourth side in this charade? C.C., Limited, sent a snazzy blonde to recruit us. She may or may not have offered something as nice to Portola. But somebody else tried to stop you in that alley after you talked to Portola's man, and somebody killed Portola's guys in Greytown as well.''

He reached for a smoke as he added, ''I wish I knew who the good guys and bad guys were around here. The only way to find out is to find out.''

Gaston said, ''Merde alors, me and my big mouth! I might have known I would provoke your catlike curiosity by stating the très obvious. Let me put it another way, Dick. It does not matter who is fucking whom, with what, for whatever reason! We owe nothing to any side involved, and every side is très sneaky and très dangerous!''

Captain Gringo lit his soggy cigar and said, ''It's about to start raining again. Meanwhile, we're forted up safe and reasonably dry where nobody on any side can possibly jump us. Let's sleep on the deal.''

''Merde alors, what deal could we possibly have with anyone? Portola sent us out with a rubber check and not enough weaponry to do anything at all important. You told the blonde you did not wish to work for her side, and the third side, whoever they may be, keeps trying to kill us!''

Captain Gringo blew a thoughtful smoke ring and said, ''Portola's a prick, but he's a pro with a reputation to consider. If we do the job we agreed to do, he has to make good on the check and the bonus. He'd never be able to hire any other knockaround guys like us if we spread the word in San José that we'd been stiffed on a contract.''

''True, but to do that, we would have to get back to San José *alive!* The triple-crossing general has loaded the dice so that we can hardly do that if we even try to keep our end of the bargain, hein?''

Something warm and wet hit Captain Gringo between the shoulder blades and ran down his back. He stood up, gripping the cigar between the teeth of a defiant smile, and said, ''Yeah, El Generale will probably shit his pants when he has to pay us off. We'd better take cover. A monkey just shit on me or it's starting to rain some more.''

Gaston rose too, protesting, ''It's impossible, damm it!

Even with the guns out pobrecitos weren't supposed to have, we don't have the manpower to attack even a modest construction gang, and that blonde was running all over recruiting professional gun-slicks as well!''

''Big deal, *I* said no, didn't I? That British outfit's running scared or they wouldn't be acting so anxious. I'll tell you what they're so worried about when I scout the site and find out. Meanwhile, we've got this Maxim, plenty of dynamite, and eleven half-ass fighting men, not counting the worthless shavetail and his cook.''

''Merde alors, you are très nuts. But you are right about the weather, and at least you can't get us killed here and now, thank God!''

People stayed up late in the tropics when it wasn't raining. But after supper on a soggy night there was nothing to do but go to bed early, and Captain Gringo had neither reading nor screwing material handy in his soggy thatched shelter. Florita had built them a pretty neat little hut, so he had to let her share it with him. They had to hang their wet clothes up to dry. So it should have been lot cozier under the flannel top sheet than it really felt. But damp tobacco tasted lousy, and lying there with a hard-on next to a frigid little dame felt even worse. He knew that most of the other good-looking stuff in camp was taken. But at least Gaston got to jerk off in private in his own shelter. He decided that if Florita made any more dumb remarks about his abusing her, he'd take her up on it. There was no sense in both of them suffering, and even a cold slab remarking on what beasts men were would probably feel better than his hand, so what the hell.

He waited, listening to the rain on the thatch above them. In the dark, he tried to picture her as ugly. It didn't work. Her warm naked hip was against his thigh and he could smell the musky odor of her femininity. He wondered if she noticed how gamy *he* was, after a long steambath with no soap.

She must have felt a certain tension in the darkness, because he'd just about decided she must be asleep when she murmured, "Are you very angry with me, Señor Deek?"

"No," he lied. "I said I understood your, ah, problem."

She sighed and said, "I wish I did. I am no longer sick from eating palmetto berries, and I wish very much for to have you like me. But when I think about what you wish for to do to me, I feel all sick inside."

"There went a great idea," he muttered half to himself. Then he said, "Go to sleep. I don't want to disgust you. As a matter of fact, the whole thing sounds pretty boring. A bird or a salmon would probably wonder what in the hell we humans got out of acting so silly."

"Sí, I have never understood it myself. When I was little, I used to watch my mamacita do naughty things in her hammock when she thought I was asleep. I could never understand why she did it. She moaned and groaned and said the men were killing her, but the next night . . ."

"Hold it," he cut in with a frown. "Did you say *men,* plural? How many lovers did your mama have, Florita?"

"Oh, many. Mamacita was most popular. You see, my papacito was a charcoal burner who was away a lot and had a drinking problem when he was at home. But I still worried about my poor momacita when she sobbed and gasped under all those brutal men who came for to visit her at night."

"Hmm, how old were you when mamacita was undergoing all this torture, kitten?"

"I don't know. Very little. Mamacita was only thirty or so when she died. The padre said she died of sin. I always thought one of those men she entertained in her hammock at night must have done something bad to her with his . . . you know."

He put a comforting arm around her bare shoulders, snuggled her head against his chest, and said, "I can see how your wedding night could have been a bust for all concerned. How old was the guy you married?"

She thought and said, "Seventeen, I think. I was fourteen

and most afraid, even though my relatives said I had to marry someone lest I become an old maid. I tried to be brave, Señor Deek, but he hurt me and made me cry. We were not married long. As I told you, he called me bad names and left me for a wicked older woman of sixteen.''

He chuckled and said, "He sounds like a real Don Juan."

He felt a tear on his bare chest. He patted her shoulder and said, "Hey, I was only teasing, Florita. I really feel sorry for the both of you. You must have been desirable as hell to him, and he was just a kid who probably didn't know how to warm a woman up first."

"Well, in fairness, my husband did not know about eating palmetto berries first. Do you think that was what we should have done, Señor Deek?"

"No. Getting poisoned or even drunk isn't the answer, Querida. You'd have been a problem for an experienced lover, once you'd been scared that way by things you were too young to understand."

"Sí, I was most uneasy when my husband tore my clothes off and threw me on the bedding. What would this experienced man have done, Señor Deek?"

He ran an exploratory hand over her breasts, gently, as he explained, "Well, he'd have let you get used to the idea first. Does this feel very frightening?"

She said, "Sí, it makes my heart pound very hard. Are you going to attack me now?"

He said, "No," as he started gently massaging her slightly smaller left breast. He didn't know why the smallest one was usually the most sensitive, but why fight nature? He moved into a better position and as he played with her now turgid nipple he kissed her cheek, moved his lips to her ear, and tongued it teasingly. She giggled and said, "Oh, that makes me feel so funny! For why are you kissing me there?"

He moved farther aboard to kiss her lush lips. She kissed back lousy. He kissed down her chin and throat as she protested that he was tickling her, and as he took her breast in his open mouth he slid the hand he'd aroused it with down her smooth belly to home plate.

She stiffened and crossed her thighs on his wrist as he soothed, "Easy, easy, just seeing if you're all there."

She opened her thighs with a resigned sigh and said, "Now you are going to have your way with me, no?"

He kissed his way back up to her mouth as he began massaging her between her trembling thighs. He kept his lips touching hers as he murmured, "No. You're not ready for that. Relax, Floritia. I'm not going to do anything yet."

She giggled and unconsciously moved her pelvis to a more welcoming angle as she asked, "What do you call what you are doing to me, if it is not anything?"

"It's called foreplay. Old exotic custom I learned from Yanqui brujas in mysterious porch swings. You can yell if I'm hurting you."

She said, "It does not hurt. It just feels silly. What are *you* getting out of playing with me so? Don't you wish for to shove more important matters in and out of me? I told you I did not really mind anymore."

He kissed her some more to shut her up. He noticed her kisses, while still unskilled, were improving as she relaxed and warmed to the occasion. He had her clit standing at attention as he rocked it in the boat, too, and she was starting to lubricate pretty good down there as she started to squirm in his arms, still more confused than passionate.

They came up for air and she murmured, "I don't think I would mind very much if you went all the way now. Your gentle hand has made me feel, ah, less frightened."

A boor would have mounted her now. He knew better. This wasn't really what you could call breaking in a virgin, even though the poor little dope had no idea what it was supposed to feel like. In a way, she was a tougher challenge than a willing virgin would have been. He knew he had to overcome more than inexperience. The poor little dame knew sex only as a frightening duty to which women were required to submit.

So he finger-fucked her all the way to climax as she squirmed, moaned, and acted a lot like her mamacita must have in times gone by. He kept his frightening parts clear of her writhing flesh as he kissed her and tongued her at her moment of orgasm. Then, as she went limp with a shuddering sigh of astounded contentment, he murmured, "Now I'm going to do it some more, with just a little of me helping my fingers, all right?"

She agreed, but started to stiffen up as he eased into the saddle. He said, "Easy now. I'm not going in until you want me to," as he rubbed the tip up and down in her love-slicked opening. She gasped and asked, "Is that your . . . you know? It feels even better than your fingers and your fingers felt ever so nicer than anything else I have ever felt down there. Was that what the other women call coming, Señor Deek?"

"Yeah. Did you like it?"

"It felt better than anything I have ever felt in my life. I can see, now, that mamacita was not really in pain after all! But why did I moan so when it felt so *good*, Señor Deek?"

"Beats me. Some dames laugh. I guess you're just supposed to make *some* damn sound at such times, and you'd sound even dumber reciting a poem."

She started moving her hips as he toyed with them both until he was hurting bad, too. Then, as he started moving it in a fraction of an inch with each of her responding thrusts, Florita suddenly sobbed, "Oh, stop teasing me and *do* it, Señor Deek!"

So he did. She hissed in mingled fear and passion as she felt him fill her to the brim. And then she raised her knees, locked her ankles atop his naked buttocks, and gasped, "I am getting that marvelous feeling again. I do not feel disgusted. I feel wonderful! Is this what fucking is supposed to feel like, Señor Deek?"

That was too dumb a question to answer orally. So he replied by coming with her. As they went limp in each other's arms, Florita said, "You have made me so happy. That felt lovely and I am so glad you have made a real woman out of me at last. I only wish it did not have to end so soon.''

He kissed her and asked, ''What's this *soon* crap? It's not eight o'clock yet and we've got all night ahead of us.''

''My God, is it possible to do it more than once?''

''Why not? You've already come twice and I'm just getting started. Let's stop for a smoke and then we'll try some other positions.''

They did. They didn't run out of positions until well after midnight, and she would have tried it flying, if they'd had wings. But he knew the sun would rise at six o'clock, and a guy needed at least six hours' sleep if he meant to carry a machine gun far enough to matter through a hot sticky jungle. So he told her they'd get to do it all over again the following night, and, once she stopped, Florita fell right to sleep, limp and purry as a well-stroked pussy cat.

He had a little more trouble falling asleep. She hadn't been bad, but it was beginning to look like he'd created a monster. He wondered what would become of Florita when the time came to ditch her. It was hard to fall asleep with a guilty conscience. And the poor little creature was going to feel betrayed, now that she'd told him more than once how much she loved him and how she meant to be his adelita forever.

Of course, a lot of people said dumb things when they were coming. He didn't remember making any promises in return. But, on the other hand, he sure hadn't told her he *hated* her while she'd been giving him her all and then some.

He told himself to forget it as the rain pattered down around them in the warm darkness. He tried to tell himself Florita was at best as deep a thinker as a friendly dog, and that none of the other pobrecitos El Generale had issued them to lose in the jungle expected to be treated as well as a valuable horse. But it wouldn't work. He couldn't help thinking of them all as human beings who trusted and depended on him.

He growled up into the unfeeling darkness, ''Okay, God. You've stuck me with a bunch of poor dumb kids and I have to do my damnedest for them. But, no shit, God, I sure could use some inspiration about now! Just between You and me, old buddy, I haven't any fucking idea how I'm going to get us out of this mess!''

Captain Gringo got a little restless sleep and woke at dawn to see that the sunrise had been canceled until further notice. The rain had been replaced by a gray flannel fog. It didn't look like it planned to go anyplace in the near future. The trade winds had either died completely or decided to skip over the low swamplands west of the coastal cuestas. Visibility was maybe ten feet, if one squinted.

He could see Florita sleeping next to him. He didn't wake her up. He couldn't think of any positions they hadn't already tried, and between the sex and the restlessness of the night just past, he wasn't looking forward to a day's march, given the strength he still felt.

He hauled on his clammy duds. It was amazing how cold one could feel in a tropical jungle when one wasn't streaming sweat from every pore. That was one of the reasons people died a lot down here. Next to yellow jack, pneumonia was the bug you had to worry about most in this grotesque clime.

He strapped on his shoulder rig, put his jacket on over it, and rolled out of the hut quietly to avoid the morning quickie Florita would doubtless demand. He found his way by homing instinct and feel to where Morales should have started the morning grub fire. All he found was a big black puddle of damp ash and char. He hunkered down and started to build a fire. It wasn't easy. There was plenty of fuel piled nearby. But the palmetto fronds were damp and the windfall faggots the peones had gathered for the cook were punky and even wetter.

But, thanks to blundering into those guerrillas, they now had more ammo to spare than matches. So he wiped a palmetto blade more or less dry on his pants, roughed out a splintery depression with his pocketknife, and pulled the slugs from a couple of rifle rounds with his teeth. He poured the powder on the palmetto blade, covered it with punk rubbed to powder between his palms, covered that with grass stems and twigs, and struck a match to see what would happen.

It worked. It took some praying and blowing, but in the end he got enough of a fire going to pile on more substantial stuff. He rose and groped his way to the tarp-covered supplies. Gaston joined him as he'd just found some coffee and was wondering what the hell to perk it in. Gaston said, "Morales will be here to do that in a moment. I just kicked the species of slugabed awake. I was about to do the same for you when I smelled the fire. I have been up for hours. Minutes, at any rate. I find it disturbing to sleep with only my hand for company."

Captain Gringo didn't comment on Gaston's sex life as they sat on the sand near the fire, letting it bake at least their fronts dry. They lit smokes. Gaston said, "I might have known you wouldn't tell me how Florita is in the feathers. I don't suppose you'd like to loan her out for a while? We are obviously not going to be able to leave this soggy hammock until this fog lets up, hein?"

Captain Gringo said, "We have to. We're already behind schedule. I want to finish the damn job and enjoy that bonus up in the high country with dry socks on for a change."

Gaston snorted in disgust and said, "I wish you would not say such silly things, my stubborn child. I have been thinking about El Generale's threats. They probably carry as much weight in Costa Rica as this rubber check I carry in a rubber for some reason."

Captain Gringo said, "I don't think it'll bounce. I've been thinking about how the hell Portola could have managed a cashier's check in the field. He must have had it made out, with the name blank, when he left León. Someone higher up gave him orders to use it as a bribe, hire guys like us, or whatever. He was telling the truth about León wanting that dam taken out.''

"Perhaps. El Generale himself could not care less. He is merely going through the motions for his superiors. If he was sincere, he would have given us real guides and not saddled us with a useless aide and other bad odds. Try it this way. El Generale is secretly opposed to taking out the dam his superiors told him to do something about?''

Captain Gringo shook his head and said, ''I think he just doesn't give a shit, despite his speech about the poor Indians. George Armstrong Custer was always making speeches back east about some guy called Lo, the poor Indian. The junta's orders struck him as a pain-in-the-ass distraction, and meanwhile he has the Granada army to worry about. So he threw us at the problem, not caring one way or the other, and hoping that whatever we did would distract the Granadines, since they ought to be between us and him about now.''

Gaston grimaced and said, ''I wish you hadn't said that. If Portola drives the other side *back,* where does that leave us?''

"Moving south a lot. Fast. Look at the bright side. The Costa Rican border patrols will be having too much trouble preventing a beaten army from crossing the border to worry about us and a handful of peones, right?''

"You intend to take these probrecitos with us, Dick?''

"If we have to. We sure as shit can't leave them lose in the jungle. We have to either do the job and let them go back to their village with El Generale's approval, or we have to add them to the population of Costa Rica without Costa Rica noticing.''

Gaston thought. Then said, ''Eh bien. Let's save ourselves a lot of trouble and just start running for the border as soon as this fog lifts. We most obviously can't lead anyone anywhere in a waist-high swamp full of soup of the pea.''

"You're right about the fog. Wrong about the direction. Don't you have any sense of curiosity, Gaston?''

"Merde alors, if I even had a sense of direction I'd know which way Costa Rica is. What is there to be curious about?

We agreed this expedition is just a side issue to El Generale and a great pain in the ass to you and me, non?''

"I want to find out what the *stinger* is. At least somebody on the ruling junta doesn't want that dam built. Somebody important in Greytown wants it built bad enough to send blondes to seduce hired guns to ride shotgun on the project. Somebody else is murdering people on both sides. That's the part I'm really curious about. I never did say no to the strawberry blonde. So it couldn't have been her people who tried to take you in that alley while she was, ah, recruiting me. It couldn't have been Portola's guys either. You hadn't said no to them.''

"True. But were our mysterious thugs trying to prevent us from going to work for the British construction company or from going to work for El Generale?''

"I don't know. That's why it's such an interesting puzzle. Meanwhile, we're not going to solve it sitting here smoking cigars. I'm going to scout to the west and see how much farther it is to dry ground. Feel like a morning stroll, Gaston?''

"Mais non; I feel like breakfast. Morales should be here any minute. Join us for breakfast, and with luck the fog will lift as well, hein? I am not sure a boy your age should be playing in the puddles out of my sight. That swamp is très dangereux even when one can see one's hand before one's eyes, Dick. No shit of the bull, don't try it in this fog.''

Captain Gringo got to his feet, saying, "The poor visibility makes it safer in some ways. I don't have to lug the Maxim or even a rifle, if nobody can see far enough to hit anything at pistol range. I'll just go out a little ways. If all I meet is more of the same, I'll come back and we'll stay here until the fog lifts. If there's dry land within a mile, I'll come back and herd you all across.''

As he moved away, Gaston called after him, "Wait until I have at least some coffee and I'll go with you, damm it!''

But Captain Gringo just kept walking. He could have used that coffee, too. But he was wide awake and restless now. He wanted to know what his plans for the day were before he settled down for grub.

The swamp was spookier than ever, now that you couldn't see much either on or below the scummy surface. The sun wasn't casting shadows in any particular direction to navigate by. Captain Gringo had a good sense of direction, but this was a little much. He fumbled in his jacket pocket and took out the little tin compass he'd hoped he still had. It was little more than a toy he'd picked up a while back to cheer the pretty lady selling junk in the Greytown market. But at least the needle pointed north. He was sort of surprised about that. He'd thought north was over *that* way.

Palming the little compass, he took a bearing on the farthest bole he could make out to the west and headed for it. The water seemed to shallow a little by the time he reached it, took a bearing on yet another tree in the middle distance, and headed for it. He grinned as he noticed the water was indeed now swishing around his knees. Dry land seemed to be nearer than he'd figured. He repeated the process with compass and trees until the black water gave way to scummy black muck. He growled, "Come on, swamp, make up your *mind*." The mud flat he was crossing, or trying to, was harder going than the swamp itself. The humic acid in the slime kept anything more advanced than vomit-green algae from growing on the slippery surface. His mosquito boots sank ankle-deep in the muck, and when he pulled a foot out of the goo it sounded and smelled like a farting elephant.

He bulled on. At least he didn't have to worry about alligators and snakes on this mud flat. He saw a wall of reeds ahead, looming in the fog. That meant more water or the edge of the swamp. He'd left his machete in camp. But if the reeds were just a hedge, a football block ought to punch him on through.

He charged into the reeds, busted through to the other side, and staggered out across more slimy muck a good six paces before he got stuck. Then, as the slimy muck reached his knees, he froze in place, looked down, and muttered, "Oh boy, now you've done it, you silly son of a bitch!"

Even standing still, he was slowly sinking. He couldn't tell if he'd blundered into muck over quicksand or just unusually soft goo. It didn't matter about the geology. He was up to his thighs now!

He twisted to look wistfully back at the reeds he'd pushed through. They were too far. He tried moving that way anyway. It made the scummy goo rise faster. By the time he gave up, his crotch was buried. A wave of panic swept over him and he yelled out in mindless fear. Then he shuddered, got a grip on himself, and growled, "Easy now. You got into this alone and you have to get out of it alone. You're too far from camp for anyone to hear and . . . hey!"

He drew his .38 and fired three shots in the air. He waited, counting to ten, then fired twice more. Three shots were the recognized distress call, but Gaston would know, too, that men who lived active lives didn't pack a six-gun against their chests with a live round under the hammer of a double-action.

He reloaded. He kept the gun out but didn't fire again just yet. The muck was up to his waist now. How fast was it inching up him? Too fast, if anyone expected to find more than his hat floating on a big bubbly puddle of black goo!

The muck was to his rib cage when he heard the sound of farting elephants coming his way and shouted, "Over here! Watch your step! I'm stuck in quicksand!"

Somewhere in the fog a gun roared three times, and three slugs ticked through the reeds to send up inky gobs of muck too close to Captain Gringo for comfort!

He snapped, "Bastard!" and fired back blindly.

The unknown on the far side of the reeds sent two more shots his way as Captain Gringo replied in kind. Then it got very quiet in the foggy swamp as both of them had to stop and reload. The muck was almost to Captain Gringo's armpits now. He remembered hearing somewhere that a guy could sort of swim in quicksand if he bit the bullet and forced himself to lie flat in the shit. But if he did that he wouldn't be able to fire back. So if the bastard trying to nail him poked a head through the reeds to see him floundering in the mud like a pig . . .

A distant voice called out, "Dick? Where are you?" and Captain Gringo called back, "Over here! Watch it! Aside from quicksand, there's some son of a bitch with a gun in the neighborhood!"

He braced himself for more slugs aimed in the direction of his voice. But all he heard was another series of elephant farts, either coming or going. It was hard to tell, the way sound echoed in the trees and fog.

He'd either hit bottom or the muck didn't want what was still floating above his outspread upper arms. So he was still head and shoulders above the surface when Gaston poked his own head through the reeds, grinned, and said, "I told you not to play in the puddles without me."

"Watch your ass, damm it. I was only doing half the shooting you heard."

"Oui, I can tell a .38 from a .45. There is nobody about but we très adorable chickens at the moment. Don't go away. I'll find a pole, hein?"

A few minutes later Gaston had. As he braced himself at one end of the gumbo-limbo sapling he'd pulled from the mud, roots and all, Captain Gringo hauled himself out of the trap hand over hand. As he joined Gaston on the relatively dry land, which was still ankle-deep slime, he sniffed and asked, "Do you smell what I smell, Gaston?"

"Aside from frog shit? Oui, when one follows people to assassinate them it is not a good idea to do so smoking violet tobacco, non? May *I* have him, or do you wish to flip a coin for the lieutenant?"

"Hold the thought for now. El Generale could consider knocking off his observer a breach of contract, you know."

"Merde alors, Dick! The depraved species of a stinkard just tried to murder you!"

"Well, he doesn't know that we know it. By now he'll be

back in camp, looking innocent. Let's play along with him until we figure out *why* he just pegged those rounds at me.''

"Sacrebleu, I have heard women were curious. I have heard cats were curious. But you, my curious child, are a species of too much! Who *cares* why a man is trying to kill one, once one knows he wants one dead?"

"Come on. We can't ask anyone to pack heavy loads through this fog and quicksand too. We're stuck until the fog lifts. Mum's the word on the pistol play for now. Ought to be interesting to watch bugs squirm on the pin while we enjoy a leisurely breakfast, right?''

There wasn't any breakfast to enjoy and everybody was acting more like chickens with theirs heads cut off than bugs on pins when they got back to the hammock. The gunfire had aroused the camp, of course. But it didn't look like anyone in sight had followed Gaston out into the swamp to see what was going on. Everybody's pants were dry.

Lieutenant Vallejo's *boots* were even dry as he sat on a pile of supplies by the cook's fire, smoking one of his perfumed cigars and pouting. As Captain Gringo and Gaston joined him, Vallejo said, "I can't find Sergeant Morales anywhere. Was he out in the swamp with you two?"

The two soldiers of fortune exchanged glances. Captain Gringo said, "He might have been. Are you missing a box of cigars as well as your private cook?"

Vallejo looked up blankly. Captain Gringo had naturally rinsed the crud off in the deeper swamp water on the way back, but he still squished when he moved. He added, "Do you have an extra pair of dry boots, lieutenant?"

Vallejo shook his head and said, "Even if I did, your feet are much bigger than mine. What's going on? What's all this about Morales and my cigars? I mean no disrespect, captain, but you are not making much sense this morning."

The tall American called Nogales over and said, "Put a

couple of the adelitas to work preparing breakfast. Tell them to make the coffee strong and black. I want everyone awake and on their toes when this fog lifts.''

Nogales saluted self-consciously and trotted away to round up a kitchen detail. Gaston chuckled and said, ''Give them a little rifle drill during trail breaks and, voilà, soldiers of the half-ass species, non?''

Vallejo pouted, ''I don't want to eat peon cooking. Where's my regular army cook?''

Captain Gringo said, ''Over the hill. Through the swamp, at any rate. He probably had a lot on his mind.''

Vallejo swore and said, ''I told him to forget that cheating wife of his, damm it!''

''Oh boy, you told him she was a cheat?''

''Why not? It was a matter of common knowledge. Man to man, didn't *you* enjoy her favors the night I sent her to your tent? Half the staff of El Generale must have had Dulcenita by now. I don't know why Morales couldn't see she was a puta.''

Florita and a girl called Luisa came over to the fire and started breakfast. Luisa was a dog. Florita looked prettier with that secretive little Mona Lisa smile she had on this morning.

The two soldiers of fortune took a walk to have a private talk as the adelitas worked and Vallejo went on pouting. Gaston said, ''Eh bien, one down and one to go. I wish it *had* been the lieutenant. He eats as much as any three of the others and refuses to either work or carry his own load.''

''Forget El Generale's pet for now. Do you think Morales is gone for good?''

Gaston shrugged and replied, ''Unless you hit him. In the fog, I could see nothing four or five meters away as I floundered toward the sounds of your dramatiques. If he caught a lucky round, he is under the mud by this time. If not, he would be miles from here by now, non?''

''I hope he's either down or trying to get back to his wife. I don't really need a pissed-off husband laying for me out there in the shrubbery wearing horns and a gun!''

"Relax. *I* laid his wife too. He knows he has other targets back with the main column, and his woman is there as well. I think that would be his main destination, thanks to the lieutenant's big mouth. You were just a target of opportunity when he found you stuck in quicksand so très tempting, hein?"

"Maybe. We're going to have to keep a sharp lookout for more than snakes and 'gators now. Let's go back for coffee and grub."

They did. The coffee was good. The Moors and Christians the peon girls had whipped up with beans and rice, while predictable and boring, stuck to the ribs. When they'd eaten, the fog was still haunting them. So Gaston spent the morning drilling the troops, if that was what one wanted to call eleven bewildered-looking guys who had trouble telling their left feet from their right feet and referred to rifle rounds as "brass Cigarillos." Gaston already had them more or less convinced that .30-30s worked best if one loaded them in the clip all facing the same way. There was no way to tell if they had any idea what he meant by lining up the sights on a distant target. There were no distant targets, and if there had been they couldn't spare the ammo and risk the noise of even modest target practice. Half the men had at least fired muzzle-loading hunting muskets in their time. So, if push came to shove, they could probably figure on at least one ragged volley before they got too confused.

The fog burned off around noon. So Captain Gringo loaded them up and moved them out. The improved visibility was purchased at the cost of hot-as-hell, naturally. But they were behind schedule and he knew that when it was cool enough to breathe in this swamp, you couldn't see where you were going.

They swung south, well clear of the quicksand trap, of course, so they couldn't check to see if Morales or any visible parts of him lay in the muck up that way. It was about three in the afternoon when they hit the wall of tangled underbrush marking the edge between mud flats and higher ground. It took an hour's machete work, taking turns in the lead, before they'd hacked their way into more open rain forest. The going was much easier after that. The shaded surface between the mossy buttress roots of the jungle giants was covered with a carpet of rotten leaves and mushrooms, which made for easier walking, if you allowed for what felt like slipping on a banana peel from time to time.

Vallejo wanted to stop and rest as soon as they were out of the swamp. Captain Gringo said his balls were sweating too, and added that they would stop when they couldn't see anymore. Whatever the moon would be up to after sundown, it would be too dark to move under the heavy rain-forest canopy. Even in broad daylight they were marching through a cathedrallike gloom. The temperature was still way to warm for comfort, but they could already feel an improvement as they marched farther from the sticky swamp in the still damp but much drier shade of the gently rising jungle.

Captain Gringo was packing the Maxim on one shoulder. So, although he was stronger than most men, he could judge when it was getting tedious to pack supplies. He allowed short trail breaks once an hour. Nobody but the self-indulgent young officer, who'd yet to carry much more than his side arms and that silly tasseled hat, bitched much when he whistled everybody upward and onward. Vallejo made up for it by bitching like a spoiled debutante with a stone in her glass slipper. Gaston, bringing up the rear guard, got to miss most of it, the lucky bastard.

Vallejo was complaining that the slope was getting steeper when Captain Gringo hissed, "Shut up and hit the dirt!" As the lieutenant just stood there looking dumb, the tall American kicked his feet out from under him and, as the lieutenant fell on his ass, waved at the men behind him to take cover. They did so, silently, bless them, as Captain Gringo moved forward, leaned the machine gun over a fallen log, then vaulted the log to move on, drawing his .38 as he strained his ears.

He heard the familiar whip crack again. He zeroed in on

the direction. It was coming from his left. He moved that way in a running crouch. He could hear the bawl of cattle and an occasional shout now. He spotted a wall of underbush on a rise ahead. He nodded and ran up to it. Then he stopped and dropped to his knees to burrow cautiously through.

As he'd expected, he found himself gazing down at a cattle drive. The vaqueros were using a sunken but open trail that wasn't supposed to be around here, according to the map. He watched long enough to see that the riders with the popping drovers' whips were obviously driving the herd to the coast to the east. Then, as he spotted a yellow mongrel trotting beside a rider on a pinto, Captain Gringo crawfished back through the brush, sprang to his feet, and made tracks. He leaped back over the log he'd leaned the Maxim against, hoisted the machine gun into position atop the log, and armed it as Vallejo asked what the hell was going on.

The tall American said, "Nothing, if their dogs don't pick out the smell of my socks. Hopefully there's enough cow in the air to keep their noses busy. There's a herd on its way to market. Maybe to Greytown by way of the crossing to the south we couldn't use. Less hopefully, they could be driving the beef to a guerrilla army over that way. It all depends on whether that bunch we shot up the other day was part of a small band or a big one."

Florita crawled up to them, dragging the extra ammo. She asked if there was anything else she could do. He smiled at her and said, "Yeah, get your pretty ass back the way it came. Get behind the biggest tree you can find. Tell anyone you run into to do the same."

"I shall stay and fight beside my soldado. That is the duty of a good adelita, no?"

"Florita, will you haul ass? Adelitas are supposed to do as they're *told,* too, goddamm it!"

She looked hurt and started crawling away. Lieutenant Vallejo followed her. Captain Gringo shrugged. He wasn't surprised, and what the hell did he need with a pretty hat right now anyway?

Captain Gringo was sighting upslope, covering them, when Gaston flopped down beside him and said, "You seem in a pensive mood, my child. Vallejo just passed me, at considerable speed for a man moving on hands and knees. He said something about cowboys, or was it Indians?"

"Light me a smoke and break open that ammo, just in case," said Captain Gringo, going on to fill Gaston in on the situation as they set up for action.

There didn't seem to be any action. It got very quiet. That didn't always mean anything. Captain Gringo moved in on people he'd spotted as quietly as he could, too. After a while a howler monkey commented from the trees ahead and a parrot answered, not sounding too excited. Captain Gringo said, "Man this weapon. I'm moving up for another look-see."

He did. When he came back he was smiling. He said, "The trail's clear. They must have been simple vaqueros after all. Better yet, the cattle trail leads due east and west. It's broad, hard-packed, and has plenty of cover on either side. Need one say more?"

Gaston sighed and said, "I knew you'd run my poor derriere off before sunset," and got to his feet.

Captain Gringo said, "Hold it. You're right about how late it is. I want to make sure no chuck-wagon crew is following that herd well behind the dust. We'll camp right here for the night and hit the trail at dawn. No fires after dark, of course. So let's get supper and some shelters built poco tiempo."

The night passed uneventfully except for Florita trying to screw him to death. The next day went well for a change, too. As Captain Gringo had hoped, the cattle trail led to cattle country. They followed it up to windswept savanna, dissected by jungle-choked canyons that the packed red earth of the cattle trail avoided in a series of ever-climbing clever hairpin turns. The sky was overcast, but the trade winds were dry and cool. It was easy to keep the expedition moving and out of trouble. Gaston had a couple of promising would-be soldados who enjoyed playing scout, and, as it was not good ambush country, he and Captain Gringo let them play at scouting the draws ahead while they checked them out for obvious idiocy.

Captain Gringo called short trail breaks from time to time and let them break long enough to enjoy a cold noon meal. But when Lieutenant Vallejo asked when they were going to siesta, Captain Gringo said they weren't, explaining, "There's not much point in napping through the hottest time of the day when it's not really hot. I want to take advantage of this open high ground to make up for the time we've lost. The map says we'll probably run into rougher-going manana."

Vallejo said, "I'm not used to hiking so far without my afternoon nap, damm it."

Captain Gringo shifted the heavy machine gun to his other shoulder and said, "My heart bleeds for you. How did you ever get that soldier suit you were wearing when we first met? Did your mommy buy it for you?"

He turned away and moved on before Vallejo could come up with the answer. Florita scampered along beside him, lugging her pack and the ammo. Considering how much of the night her legs had been spread apart, she was still legged up better than the so-called infantry officer staggering and bitching behind her.

From time to time as the trail hairpinned higher Captain Gringo had a good look at the others, with Gaston bringing up the rear. They were all soldiering well, despite the heavy loads some of them were packing. By the time the darkening overcast above them warned that the sun was setting, wherever the hell it was, they'd crested the long slope. Captain Gringo saw miles of much the same kind of country ahead, leading downward out of sight in the dark mists. He stepped off the trail, braced the Maxim in the fork of a wind-twisted thorn tree, and called out, "This is where we camp for the night, muchachas y muchachos."

They didn't have to be told twice. But he noted with

approval that his porters gathered all the supplies close in before the men flopped to the grass and the women started setting up camp.

Gaston joined Captain Gringo, muttering, "Merde alors, my legs are getting old for this sort of business." He looked around and added, "Eh bien. There's no water, running or otherwise. There's firewood, but not enough thatch for lean-tos. If we spread our bedding on the grass and it decides to rain again . . ."

Captain Gringo shrugged and said, "We'll get wet. But what the hell, the trades are sweeping across this ridge pretty good, so we'll dry out."

He saw some women building a fire and called out, "Hey, muchachas, make it bigger. After dark I don't want open flames up here atop this ridge. So let's get plenty of coals going for bedtime coffee, eh?"

He stared out across the open slopes all around them, nodded, and said, "We'll pile the supplies in a circle around us and bed down close together. There's nobody in sight for a good five miles, and it'll be dark soon. But why take chances? You want to take the first guard mount, Gaston?"

Gaston nodded. Then, noticing that Lieutenant Vallejo had wandered off to get his own roll from the porter packing it, Gaston asked, "Doesn't that species of young squirt get to pull guard at all, Dick?"

"Would *you* like to trust him with your ass while both of us were in the sack?"

"Forget what I just said. I'll put four reasonably bright-looking pickets out and hold the fort until midnight. Do you think you can get all the screwing you need by then?"

Captain Gringo chuckled and said, "I may even get an hour's sleep. Don't forget to whistle, cough, or something as you approach my trundle bed."

"Oh, dear, I wanted to watch. I don't suppose you'd like to, ah, fix me up with that precocious child you'll be leaving in that warm bedroll?"

"I would if I thought she'd go for it, old buddy. I don't think she would. She's, ah, sort of romantic."

"How droll. But far be it from me to come between happy honeymooners. At least my fist still loves me."

By the time they'd seen to setting up camp and had eaten supper, the lights had gone out as if someone had pulled a switch in the sky. Thanks to the overcast, it was black as a bitch away from the ruby glow of the cook-fire coals. Knowing he'd be up from midnight to dawn, Captain Gringo turned in with no further bullshit. Florita beat him into the bedroll and out of her clothes. She pleaded with him to hurry as he made sure the Maxim was comfy in its tarp at the head of the bedroll. He draped his clothes and shoulder rig over it. Then he draped himself over Florita and they went deliciously nuts together for a while. Their bedroll was inside the ring of supplies, but far enough from any other for them to get away with a modest amount of acrobatics in private. He asked her to keep her orgasmic groans down to a roar and she tried. By now the others all knew they were an item anyway.

They made love for an hour or more and then Captain Gringo actually managed to catch some sleep. It didn't feel like he'd had much when Gaston approached, singing the Marseillaise in a sardonic tone. Captain Gringo sat up, told him to shove a sock in it, and started dressing as Gaston explained that he'd already rousted out and positioned the four pickets for the last watch. He added, "I did not feel it wise to strain their brains with nonsense about pass words and countersigns, hein? I told them not to shoot at anyone approaching from inside our lines and vice versa. It should be good practice for them. Anyone approaching a barricaded camp across open ground is obviously going to be an idiot, or a cow."

The little Frenchman's prattle had Florita half-awake and begging to be abused some more. So Captain Gringo told Gaston to shut up and told the girl to go back to sleep. They both obeyed him. He got up, stamped his feet solidly in his boots, and checked his .38 as he started his rounds. Gaston didn't go with him.

Captain Gringo found the four still-sleepy peones where Gaston had posted them to cover the camp north, south, east, and west. He warned each man to stay awake and listen to the crickets. As long as the crickets sang in the grass all around, nothing important was moving out there. If they heard the crickets switch off, they were to shoot first and ask questions later. The dramatic orders seemed to jar them a bit more awake. That had been the general idea.

Like all old soldiers, good or bad, Captain Gringo found guard duty second only to K.P. as one big pain in the ass. Officers didn't have to pull K.P. but they still got to stand guard, so that made guard duty their biggest pain in the ass. But, unlike scrubbing pots and pans, guard duty was not a duty one could safely dope off on. Nine hundred and ninety-nine times out of a thousand, standing guard was just boring as hell. But doping off that one time in a thousand could kill you. He tried to remember that as he walked up and down in the clammy darkness, smoking and trying to stay alert. It wasn't easy, even for a good soldier.

He was uncomfortably cool in his tropic linen jacket, this late at night on a windswept ridge. He couldn't help remembering how cozy and warm it was in that bedroll with Florita. He couldn't help wondering if anyone would know, and if it would really hurt, if he sort of posted himself under the covers with her. He'd still be awake, after all, and the four pickets on guard would spot anything he was liable to see in this blackness.

He didn't give in to temptation. Rank had its privileges. But rank had its responsibilities too. He found a tree, got on the lee side of the trunk, out of the trades, and hunkered down to smoke a little more comfortably before it was time to walk the line again. He was between the south and west pickets, staring out into the darkness of the unknown land ahead of them, should morning ever come. The crickets were serenading him. A mosquito took advantage of the still air behind the tree near the ground to sting his cheek. He slapped it absently. The slap knocked the cigar from his mouth. He blinked in mild surprise at his own sleepy reflexes and leaned over to grope for the smoke glowing in the grass. At that moment a burst of machine-gun fire swept the area, including the area his head had just occupied!

Captain Gringo rolled away from the chopped-up tree, whipping out his .38 and cursing as all hell booke loose around him in the dark. People were screaming, the machine gun was chattering like an insane metallic woodpecker, and the tall American flat in the grass was disoriented for the moment as he had to adjust his thinking. Enemies were supposed to attack from that way, not *that* way, damm it!

Then he located the source of all the automatic fire by the stuttering orange glow and pegged a shot at it. He saw what a lousy notion that had been when the machine gun traversed his way and spewed a humming horde of angry metal bees over him as he hugged the dirt.

But two or more could play at the same game, and he could tell by the cough of another .38 that Gaston was still alive and hadn't forgotten to write.

The machine gun groped for Gaston in the dark as the Frenchman ducked and rolled away from his own muzzle flash. So Captain Gringo rose like a flipper on its fins and pegged another three rounds of rapid pistol fire before rolling over three times and pressing his cheek bone into the dirt as he reloaded by feel. The machine gun, meanwhile, fell silent. The darkness still seemed to tingle to its chatter and the air reeked with the acrid scent of cordite, although, when he really listened, all he heard was someone moaning something dumb about his mother.

Gaston's voice called out from the distance, "Dick?" and when Captain Gringo called back, "Yo?" the Frenchman replied, "I think they left by the north door. There's a picket here who doesn't seem to be breathing anymore."

Captain Gringo leaped to his feet and ran that way in a low crouch. He joined Gaston by the guard, who lay face down and bloody in the grass. Gaston said, "They went thataway as you Yanks put it so crudely. From the dulcet tones of their running footsteps, I make it two men. The question before the house now is whether they brought their own machine gun or used ours, non?"

Captain Gringo swore and tore for his own bedroll, tripping over someone's corpse in the dark, but managing to stay on his feet until he dropped to his knees by Florita and reached to shake her to her senses. She didn't answer. He got a palm slicked with blood. When he struck a match, he saw why. Florita was staring owlishly up at him with three wide eyes. Her own and the big fried egg of blood and brains in the middle of her forehead.

The Maxim that should have been in its tarp beyond her shattered head was gone. He stared at the flat expanse of canvas tarp, covered with spent shells, and cursed as the match burned down to his fingers. Gaston had joined him just in time to take in the messy scene. Gaston said, "Eh bien, we shall call the roll and see who is dead or missing, non?"

Captain Gringo had noticed a Krag rifle in the grass nearby before the match went out. He groped for it as he told Gaston, "Haven't time. You stay here and mind the store. If they headed north they'll make for that tree-filled canyon over that way."

He checked the action of the rifle. There was a full clip of .30-30, and, what the hell, he was only after two guys. He started jogging out into the darkness as, behind him, he heard Gaston wail, "Dick, have you gone mad? It's two to one, and they have a *machine gun!*"

Gaston was like that, thought Captain Gringo as he cleared the tangled confusion of the shot-up camp and began to run faster. The old Frog meant well, but he was always telling a guy something he already knew.

The day dawned gray and clammy as a used contraceptive. When Captain Gringo was able to see far enough to matter, he was miles north of Gaston and the others, still running on high ground. Instead of plunging into the brushy canyon winding north from camp, the tall American had kept to the high open savanna it wound through. With any luck at all, by now he had to have outpaced anyone moving through the scrub below.

But if they were down there anywhere within a mile, they'd have him outlined against the sky now. So he cut right and slid down the slope on his heels and butt, holding the rifle across him at port arms, until he hit bottom.

The canyon, as he'd assumed, had a fairly open sandy water channel winding through the tangled spinach filling most of it. He dropped behind a fallen tree, still in full leaf despite its roots having been undercut by the last flash flood through this particular stretch. He levered a round into the chamber of his Krag. Then he waited. He waited at least a million years.

A bird that wasn't in any nature-study book sang a song he'd never heard before above his head. A lizard covered with emerald scales came wandering along the fallen treetrunk, darting its little licorice-whip tongue to taste the bark ahead as it sensed Captain Gringo's presence without being able to tell the exact location of the immovable object it sensed.

The distraction helped. Captain Gringo knew all too well how many an ambush went sour because somebody got impatient. Aside from the way his balls and mosquito-bitten cheek were itching, he had to fight the growing certainty that he was waiting, and waiting, for nothing much. If the guys he'd tried to cut off had made better time than anticipated along the dry hard-packed sand running down the middle . . .

"They didn't," he insisted to himself, remembering how far he'd run across the high ground above, in a straighter line. He told himself the wise-asses with the stolen machine gun wouldn't have just bolted down a strange canyon in the dark. Aside from having to hack their way at least some of the time, they'd have stopped from time to time to cover the trail behind them, in case.

Or had they? They might have assumed that, with any number of escape routes to choose from, and given the fact they had the only serious weapon for miles, nobody had been dumb enough to follow them. In that case, they could have passed this stretch by now, and as Captain Gringo crouched there like an idiot listening to birds . . .

He told himself it wouldn't hurt to move north down the sand a way and see if he could pick up any footpritns. Then he stared at the open sand in front of him and warned himself not to listen to idiots. The crust of dead flat sand he had the rifle trained on was unbroken.

But, of course, if they'd been smart enough to avoid open stretches and if they'd hugged the slopes above where the brush met dry grass . . .

"If the dog hadn't stopped to shit he'd have caught the rabbit!" Captain Gringo growled silently. It was well he did so. He'd no sooner growled the old army bromide when he heard voices coming his way from the south.

The tall American was already down and sighting the Krag. So he didn't move a muscle as he heard someone complaining, "I can't carry this all the way, señor. I have hurt my foot. I have not boots like yourself, por favor!"

A more familiar voice replied, "You will carry for me or I will kill you. *Move*, you lazy peon!"

Then they broke cover. Lieutenant Vallejo was herding the porter called Ernesto at gunpoint. Ernesto was packing the Maxim. Vallejo had another Krag's muzzle against Ernesto's floating ribs.

Captain Gringo grimaced. He'd have liked to have a longer conversation with the son of a bitch, but Vallejo's rifle was aimed right at him, through Ernesto. So Captain Gringo drew a bead on the shaded brow under the fancy tasseled brim of Vallejo's Spanish hat, and fired.

Vallejo fired too, in a mindless reflex as his brains exploded from his shattered skull. The lieutenant's body fell backward, and Ernesto fell forward, landing face down with the machine gun across the nape of his neck.

Captain Gringo moved in to survey the damage. He picked up the Maxim and brushed off the sand. Then he lay it on a patch of dry grass and rolled Ernesto over. The peon's eyes opened. In an injured tone, he said, "I think you have killed me; señor!"

"I didn't kill you. Your amigo, Vallejo, did. Shall we talk about that? You've got at least a few minutes left and you may as well spend them as comfortable as you can."

"Por favor, don't hurt me, Captain Gringo! It was all the lieutenant's fault! I told him you would catch us. He made me do it. This I swear!"

The American nodded and asked, "What was the hold he had over you?"

Ernesto said, "He knew I once deserted the army. I don't see why he cared. It was never my fight and I never asked to join any army. But he said if El Generale found out, my people would suffer and . . ."

"Skip the details. Frankly, this doesn't figure to be a long conversation, amigo. Do you know how he worked that prank on me in the swamp?"

"Sí; he was very pleased with himself and boasted to me about it. He awoke to find Morales gone. He went after Morales without waiting to put on his clothes. He saw you in trouble. He tried to help you die. When it did not work, he came back ahead of you, put on his clothes, and, as he said, made the big fool of you!"

"Okay. Did Morales get away after Vallejo filled his head with stories about his cheating wife being passed around among the officers?"

The wounded man didn't answer. He wasn't wounded anymore. He was dead. Captain Gringo closed Ernesto's eyes for him, then salvaged both the dead men's arms and ammunition before hoisting the Maxim to his shoulder and heading back. The load was a bitch and going up the steep slope was a lot rougher than sliding down it had been, but he made it.

Early as it was, the sun was burning off the morning mists now and the day figured to be a scorcher. He was sweating like a pig by the time he made it back to Gaston and the pathetic handful of survivors waiting by the piled supplies and fresh-turned mounds of red earth.

Captain Gringo dropped his load atop a canvas-covered mound and told Gaston, in English, "The lieutenant. He told us he was getting tired of walking."

Gaston nodded and murmured, "Let's keep it among us girls. I have put two and two together and already come up with a possible breach of contract if Portola wants to be silly about his observation team, hein?"

"Right. We don't know nothing. Morales must have gotten lost in that swamp. Who can say where Vallejo and Ernesto went after we got smoked up by some person or persons unknown? Where's old Nogales?"

Gaston pointed with his chin at a grave mound and said, "Four men and six women left. The other adelita we had to bury with Florita was Luisa, and she was ugly. C'est la guerre. You didn't really need to bring those rifles back, Dick. We have more guns and debris in general than six men and six women can possibly carry, non?"

"Yeah. We'll eat as big a breakfast as we can hold and only pack the absolutely essential ammo and explosives."

Gaston frowned and asked, "Don't you have that backwards, Dick? We're several hungry days and nights from the Costa Rican border, and the idea about the dam will have to be shelved, non?"

"No. With guns we can eat off the country. Now that we're down to half-a-dozen guys and maybe some tough dames, it's going to take every stick of dynamite we can carry to take that construction site out."

Gaston sighed and made the sign of the cross as he muttered, "Why did I not listen to my poor old mother when she told me I had thd makings of a good cat burglar? I keep telling us you are going to get us all killed, and, as you see, you are doing it très rapidly! Use your head, you species of stubborn bull! Now that we have been whittled down to a modest crowd, crossing the border should be no great problem, but . . .''

"Oh, shut up and let's eat, damm it," Captain Gringo cut in, adding, "The map says we should be somewhere near the headwaters of that tributary the other side wants to dam. We're not gonna get paid unless we blow it, and I'm tired of being a bum. We go back to San José with money to spend for a change or, damm it, we just ain't going.''

"That's what I just tried to tell you," said Gaston.

The next twenty-four hours were more uncomfortable than interesting. After stuffing their guts, the survivors marched downhill half the day, packing ammo, explosives, and a little coffee and rice. At noon they cut through swampy low-lying jungle for a few hours, then got to march uphill until Captain Gringo called another halt for the day atop a savanna-covered rise that looked much like the one on which they'd spent the previous night.

The male and female membership of the expedition evened out now. But Captain Gringo hadn't taken time to get next to any of the adelitas left. He was heartsick, legsore, and none of the sweaty dirty-faced mujers inspired him in particular. They brewed a pot of coffee to pass around, and he noticed that Gaston had been working on old Teresa, as the fat but still fairly pretty one was called. Captain Gringo turned in alone. He'd replaced his bloodstained bedding with odds and ends less shot up before leaving the other camp that morning. He still had trouble getting comfortable after dark. He knew it was only his imagination, or the body odor of some other adelita, that was haunting his lonely bedroll now. It bothered him anyway. But he managed to catch a few hours' sleep before Gaston shook him awake to say they had trouble.

They hadn't posted guards. Partly because they were so far out in the middle of nowhere and mostly because they all needed rest. Captain Gringo cursed himself for risking it when Gaston said two of the men and their adelitas had deserted during the night. They'd left most of their ammo behind, but they'd swiped the last of the coffee and rice.

So as they sat around the dead embers of the campfire in the morning mist, the two soldiers of fortune and their dumb or faithful remaining followers shared cigar smoke for breakfast.

The four girls and two male peones looked more frightened than hungry. Captain Gringo assured them they'd doubtless flush a deer before they starved to death, and there was no water problem in the rainy season. As if to make his point, it started to rain some more. He didn't want to get their map in worse shape than it was. So he read it from memory as he pointed southwest with his chin and said, ''You can't see it from up here, but the valley ahead is it. This rain is freshening the headwaters of the Rio Dorado and the Rio Dorado runs into the San Juan, when nobody dams it. I figure we're maybe two days' march from the dam site. We may be able to make better time rafting down the Dorado. Does anybody here know if it's navigable?''

They just stared at him dumbly from under the dripping brims of their sombreros. He nodded and said, ''That's what I thought you'd say. Bueno. We'll find out when we get there.''

Gaston had been thinking. He said, ''I have never been up the Dorado. But the name is très interesting, non?''

Captain Gringo shrugged and said, ''The old Spaniards were always expecting El Dorado around the next bend. They may have named it the 'gilded river' because there was some placer gold in it, or just because they hoped there was. There's a little color in lots of the Central American mountain streams. So far, nobody's ever found a serious mother lode.''

''True. But when one mentions gold in the same breath as one discusses vast construction activities across a streambed . . .''

''Forget it. If there was enough placer to matter near the mouth of the Rio Dorado, there'd be a Spanish ghost town instead of empty jungle there. We've got enough to worry about without abandoned gold mines, Gaston.''

''How do you know? Can you think of a better reason to indulge in très fatigue dredging and damming that nobody seems to be paying for, Dick?''

Captain Gringo let it go. Maybe if the last two porters thought they were hunting for gold they wouldn't desert right away. Captain Gringo got to his feet and said, ''Well, we're going to have to leave one box of dynamite and the extra rifles behind. There are eight of us left. Eight times forty is three-twenty and that's not enough. Okay, if the four girls pack forty each and us tough guys pack sixty . . . damn, that's not going to leave us much boom-boom when it's time to boom-boom, is it?''

Gaston said he had a better idea. Captain Gringo told him to shut up.

He got everybody loaded up and moving out before he wondered if he was really going anywhere important packing the heavy Maxim and an extra hundred pounds of gear. But what the hell. At least it was cool with the rain coming down. So he headed down slope.

The view ahead was mostly shifting veils of rain, but the grassy savanna was open and free of machete work. So they were making good time. It now seemed pointless for Gaston to bring up the rear of what was no longer a column. So the Frenchman walked at Captain Gringo's side, bitching about their going the wrong way. He pointed to their left and said, ''This ridge must run close to the San Juan and the border, non? Wait, before you say boring things about a deal being a deal, let us consider that we have tried as much as any reasonable general could expect!''

''General Portola isn't reasonable and he can stop that check with one wire, damm it!''

''True, if he decides to do so before we can reach the bank in San José. But who is likely to tell him he should, my quixotique reader of oral contracts? If those deserters are picked up at all, it will be days from here and now. Portola has no reason to assume we are not still trudging madly on toward the doomed dam site. If we hasten for San José, before he begins to wonder . . .''

Captain Gringo shook his head stubbornly and said, ''We can't cash that check without doing the job.''

''Don't be ridiculous, Dick. I just explained how we could.''

''Yeah? Then what? Who's going to hire a couple of soldiers of fortune after word gets around that they double-crossed a client? Besides, I want that bonus Portola promised.''

''Merde alors, to collect the bonus, we'd not only have to try for the thrice-accursed dam, we'd have to destroy it so completely that Portola and the León junta would never have to worry about it again!''

''Yeah, and I'm not sure we have enough dynamite, even if the guys at the dam site showed us where to plant it. But pick 'em up and lay 'em down, old buddy. We sure as hell can't do a thing about it till we get there.''

Gaston dropped back to talk dirty to Teresa. Captain Gringo trudged on alone on point, frowning as he heard the rumble of thunder ahead. That was all they needed now. So far, the only thing they'd escaped getting hit by was lightning. But they were on a high open slope. So how did one get off it pronto?

He swung for a brushy draw running more or less westward down the open savanna slope. He heard the crackle of . . . lightning, again. He frowned as he scanned the open sky over that way. He didn't see any sign of lightning in the ash-gray clouds ahead.

He called a halt and whistled Gaston over near the lip of the ravine. Gaston said, ''Oui, it sounds more like gunfire than thunder to me, too. What do you think we should do about it? If it were up to me, I'd of course be digging in or moving in a sensible direction. But I see you have that wicked look in your eye again.''

Captain Gringo started unloading most of the gear he was packing. He told the others to take cover in the brush below. As they did so, he checked the fit of the soggy canvas ammo belt in the Maxim, then wrapped the free end loosely around his waist. Gaston sighed and made sure there was a round in the chamber of his rifle before he told the peones to stay put and followed Captain Gringo.

They didn't duck down in the arroyo to their right. It was there for cover when and if they needed it. Meanwhile, they could move faster along the grassy rim, and nobody could see more than a city block in the falling rain in any case.

They moved downslope until a tree line loomed ahead. A rifle squibbed in the distance. Gaston nodded and said, "Oui, the firefight is taking place on the other side. Hopefully nobody is expecting anyone at all to drop in from this direction. But do we really have to, Dick? Nobody on either side ahead could possibly be anyone we're fond of!"

Captain Gringo didn't answer. He saw, as they neared the wall of trees, that it was merely a planted shelter belt. A rusty barbed-wire fence ran between the double row of cedar. Vines and other crud had of course climbed up to dangle from the three strands of wire and the patent metal termite-proof posts it was strung between. The vines offered a screen, albeit not a bulletproof one, as the soldiers of fortune eased up to it for a look beyond.

The view was interesting. Downslope was a substantial ranch house, with gunsmoke drifting from its shattered windows. Farther up the slope, backs to Captain Gringo and Gaston, a skirmish line of men in ragged khaki and crossed ammo bandoleros was peppering the ranch house from behind tree stumps and an occasional boulder. As Captain Gringo braced the Maxim across the fence, Gaston whispered, "Wait! How do we know who the good guys and the bad guys are, Dick?"

"Jesus, can't you tell banditos when you see 'em?"

"Eh bien, ragged rascals bearing arms are hardly ever anything else in these parts. But what if the ones in the house are as bad?"

"We'll have half as many to deal with," Captain Gringo

replied, as he let the ammo belt fall between his booted feet and opened up with the Maxim at point-blank range.

Sombreros, weapons, and other bits and pieces flew skyward as spine-shot men jerked one last time and died while Captain Gringo traversed the line of exposed skirmishers. One rolled over the rock he'd been behind as Maxim slugs bounced off it. So Captain Gringo missed him. But someone from the house didn't, and that was that. Captain Gringo still had half a belt left when he stopped firing. It seemed eerie, listening to the kitten-clawed raindrops all around in the sudden silence.

Finally a door opened a crack and a voice from the besieged house called out, "God bless you, whoever you are, and look out for your flanks! There were others on the far side! They seem to have ridden off, but they may not have."

Captain Gringo called back, "Gracias, amigos. Are you for Granada or León?"

"In God's truth, señor, we are not enthusiastic about either side in this long tedious civil war. We are simple rancheros who only wish for to be left alone. As you just saw, this is not always easy, even out here in the back country."

Captain Gringo leaned the still-primed Maxim against the fence and told Gaston, "Cover me. I'm going in."

"I will cover you, but you are très crazy!"

Captain Gringo wasn't sure Gaston was wrong as he eased through the fence and started for the ranch house, keeping his hands politely out to his sides as he stepped over a brain-spattered straw sombrero and stopped midway, calling out, "Is it permitted, señores?"

"Mi casa es su casa, amigo, sent by a just God in the nick of time! Do you and your people have ammunition for to sell us? We were almost out of it when you came to answer our prayers just now!"

Captain Gringo went the rest of the way. The oak door opened wider and a dignified-looking old gent stepped out, .45 politely holstered as he held out his hand and said, "I am called Javier Trujillo by white people like yourself. I allow the Indios to call me Don Javier, although in truth I do not own that much. Just the land around for a day's ride. My vaqueros left a few days ago for Greytown, for to deliver beef to the Royal Navy there. Those ladrónes must have heard there were few of us left here for to defend ourselves, eh?''

Captain Gringo said he'd spotted Don Javier's trail herd along the way, neglecting to mention that the feeling hadn't been mutual, as the old man led him inside.

The American had expected to meet the house servants and women in native costume. He was surprised by the couple in the sort of safari gear English wore for some reason in warm parts of the world. As the old rancher introduced them as a Mr. and Mrs. Palmer, who'd arrived one jump ahead of the bandit gang, Captain Gringo saw that the coast was clear for Gaston to come in. If the Latins here made a regular practice of jumping strangers, the Palmers wouldn't be looking so alive and chipper.

Excusing himself by bluntly telling the old man why, Captain Gringo stepped back outside and called out to Gaston, who broke cover and headed in, packing the Maxim. Palmer, looking over Captain Gringo's shoulder, said, "Ah, I was right about it being a machine gun you chaps were using. Do you think the ones on the far side of the house took the hint?"

Captain Gringo nodded and said something about most bandits not liking anything like even odds. But when the old man suggested sending his peones out to clean up the mess, Captain Gringo shook his head and said, "They'll keep in this cool rain an hour or so. Let's not take chances until we have a chance to do some scouting."

Palmer said something dumb about getting right to it and all that. The taller American said, "Not yet. Wait until it stops raining and we can see beyond rifle range."

Palmer said, "Oh, right. You sound like you know this business, ah, Mister . . . ?"

"Walker. Dick Walker. I'm a professional soldier. What's your line?"

"Engineer. At least, I was. My wife and I just left a construction site down the valley. Had to. The man in charge is a bloody maniac."

Captain Gringo had learned in the past, the hard way, to play with his cards close to his vest. Gaston, despite his apparent distaste for silence, could keep a few thoughts to himself when he wanted to. So a warning look as they met in the doorway was all it took. Neither soldier of fortune had any intention of discussing their reasons for being in these parts with an engineer of Consolidated Construction, Ltd., before they'd fed him a little more rope.

Don Javier sent a couple of armed ranch hands to gather in the others left upslope in the ravine. Hopefully, by the time they returned with the peones and gossip, more cards would be on the table.

They were. As old Don Javier's wife and two daughters served refreshments in the main room, before a roaring fire in the baronial fireplace, Edward Palmer, as he turned out to be called, explained how he and his wife, Ruth, had ridden north from the dam site amid considerable curses and threats. Ruth Palmer was a vapidly pretty girl with big innocent blue eyes. Her hair was now a mess, although it probably looked okay pinned up and when given a fresh henna rinse now and again. She just nodded in weary agreement to everything her husband said.

Palmer explained that their horses had given out along the way. Horses did that when one drove them as hard as the English couple apparently had in tropic heat. Captain Gringo waited until they had him up-to-date about making it here to the Trujillo rancho, with bandits chasing them, before he asked mildly, "What was that you said before about the man in charge of building that dam or whatever?"

Gaston added, "Oui, you said he was très mad. May one assume he made the, ah, pass at madame?"

Ruth Palmer fluttered her lashes and looked down at her cup. Her husband grimaced and said, "Oh, heavens, one expects a bit of that nonsense when one has a reasonable-looking wife. That's not why we left. I told Chumford, the engineer in charge, that I was resigning in protest of his unprofessional methods. Didn't mention my wife's complaints about his uncouth manners at all, as a matter of fact. We naturally meant to leave the site by riverboat. I mean, that's the way we *got* there, eh what?"

"How come you wound up here, miles out in the jungle, Palmer?"

"Had to. Chumford refused to accept my resignation. Told me I was confined to quarters till I came to my senses, or some such rot. We could hardly accept that. By Jove, we're British subjects, not perishing, ah, never mind."

"You two just grabbed a couple of broncs and rode out blind?"

"Well, I must say we rode rather fast, until the bloody brutes dropped out from under us. But I knew where we were going. We mean to report Chumford to the government in León."

Old Don Javier frowned politely and said, "Forgive me, Señor Palmer. But while I know little of the building of dams, I know my own country, and with all due respect, you never would have made it as far north as León. It is well you stumbled over us when you did. There is nothing to the north except very high hills, covered with thick timber and Indios who, alas, have very thick heads when it comes to strangers."

Palmer shrugged and said, "It's partly the Indians, and of course yourselves as well, that I have to tell the junta in León about. This entire watershed will be flooded, if and when Chumford finishes that bloody dam."

He sipped his cup, sighed, and added, "That's if things go *well*, of course. They've already built the coffer dam. So the water's backing up rapidly, thanks to this being the rainy season. But, as I kept trying to tell that maniac and his underlings, the dam will never *hold* where they've chosen to build it."

Captain Gringo and Gaston exchanged glances. Gaston asked, "In that case, what is the great danger to anyone in this valley, m'sieur? If the dam gives way, this valley will not be flooded, non?"

Palmer made an impatient gesture and said, "It's not that simple. If I read my own figures correctly, the dam will hold for a time. Perhaps a year. Maybe even more. By then, of course, this entire valley will have been drowned. The dam's designed as earth fill, covered with concrete. It will take a few earth tremors before it gives. But, as I kept trying to tell Chumford, sooner or later it will give completely, and when that happens, well, one can only hope the Good Lord has warned people all down the San Juan to build themselves a perishing great fleet or *arks!*"

Captain Gringo whistled as he got the picture. He said, "Oh boy! There are border villages on either side of the river farther down. Built close to the current water level, too!"

Palmer said, "It gets worse. If you know the lower San Juan, you know the land rises steeply north and south of the main channel. Railroad lines and navigational improvements are all placed neatly, and bloody *tightly*, between the riverbanks and hillsides. When that big dam goes, a hundred-foot wall of roaring flood will simply sweep everything, and everybody, out to sea!"

He took another sip from his cup and added, "Chumford says I'm too sentimental about a few perishing natives. Perhaps I am. But, dash it all, we are talking about human lives and property, what?"

"Welcome to the human race, Palmer," said Captain Gringo, smiling thinly. The Hispanics in the room were mercifully too ignorant of English to know how they'd been dismissed by the British dam builders, and even by Palmer to some extent.

Ruth Palmer said something earnest about them having to warn the Nicaraguan government. Captain Gringo said the junta in León already knew the danger to this valley and didn't approve of it. He added that their best bet was a run for the nearer safety of Greytown, and Don Javier said that was no problem, once his vaqueros and their mounts got back.

Captain Gringo still wasn't ready to put his own cares on the table, just in case. He'd known from the beginning that the dam across the Dorado had to go. Gaston had a more curious nature. He said, "I fail to detect a sensible motive for all this distressing dam building, M'sieur Palmer. Before you had your falling out with this churlish M'sieur Chumford, did he give any sensible reasons at all for building his très mysterious and, it now seems, temporary structure?"

Palmer shrugged and said, "There were plenty of good reasons, on paper. The plans call for hydroelectric channels, navigational locks, and so on. I knew as soon as I felt Pocopoco tremble under my very feet that the whole idea was insane."

"Pocopoco?" Captain Gringo frowned.

Don Javier said, "I know the mountain he speaks of, señor. It is a volcano, down at the far end of the valley. Los Indios named it that because that is what it sounds like when it is going poco, poco, poco, poco."

He chuckled and added, " 'Poco' may mean 'little' in my language, but in truth Pocopoco is a most impressive peak, even when it is not erupting."

Captain Gringo remembered the unnamed peak on his ordnance map and asked, "Are we talking about an active volcano, with one wing of the earth-filled dam built smack against its slopes?"

Palmer nodded and said, "I see you have heard something about the Dorado Dam. That's exactly what they're doing, or trying to. Didn't take me any time at all to see they were insane. You can feel the bloody ground shake under you eight or ten times a day near that bloody dam site! When I tried to tell Chumford, he just laughed and said it was my job to design the canal locks, as I was being paid to do that until I was blue in the bloody face, and you know the rest."

They didn't, really. It now seemed obvious to Captain Gringo that the so-called bandits attacking the house the Palmers had taken shelter in were hired guns, not your run-of-the-mill wandering ladrónes. But he kept that card to his vest, too. He wanted the old man and his people to go on sheltering the harmless runaways, no matter how their last employer felt about them.

Turning to old Don Javier, he asked how often Pocopoco was supposed to really poco seriously.

The courteous old man shrugged and said, "As my young Anglo guest says, it may lay quietly for a year, two years, perhaps three. Then, boom, El Pocopoco clears his throat, kills everyone and everything for kilometers around, and goes back to sleep again—until it goes *boom* again! No Indios can tell you more. No Indios are stupid enough to live near Pocopoco."

Palmer said, "It's a classic strata cone. Built up of layer after layer of lava and cinders, like a bloody textbook example. Told them that when I first laid eyes on what they were anchoring one wing of the dam to. Chumford said it was long extinct. Took a walk up the slope. Bloody noisy and wobbly for an extinct anything. Felt at least three tremors in an hour's walk. You know, of course, what happens when water pours into hot magma? Told Chumford that if the rising floodwaters ran down some ruddy crevice into the underground lava chambers . . . well, one reads about what happened to Krakatoa back in the eighties if one takes basic geology, what?"

There was a commotion outside. The two soldiers of fortune followed Don Javier when he went to see what was going on. His ranch hands had come back without anyone. They said that when they got to where Captain Gringo had told his people to wait, nobody had waited. He asked if the deserters had left his supplies. They said there were some boxes of ammo and dynamite they hadn't seen fit to mess with.

Gaston sighed and said, "I shall never trust a woman again. Teresa said she loved me, too! The least she could have done would have been to take the damn dynamite with her, non?''

Captain Gringo smiled thinly and said in English, "Don't get your hopes up just yet, you old goat. That talk about one end of the dam being against an active volcano gives me an idea. Remember what Palmer said about cold water and hot lava? If it was possible to blast just a little old crack in the right place . . .''

"Oh, wait for me, Teresa! I am coming, *ma chérie!* Now the child you left behind is planning to detonate volcanoes in my poor old ears!''

Captain Gringo laughed and said, "Relax. I'm not sure it'll work. We may still have to do it the hard way.''

Don Javier wouldn't hear of his honored guests grunting their own gear in off the rainy slopes no matter how noisy some of it might be. He said he prided himself on being a perfect host. He didn't have to say he was more worried about those bandits hitting again than about the comfort of his peones. He rounded up some muchachos made of sterner stuff, or dumber, anyway, and told them to go get the dynamite and ammo pronto. Gaston thought it only fair to suggest that they do so without smoking and to store it in the outbuilding farthest from the main house.

Things got even nicer when the rain let up before sundown and the sun came out just long enough to dry things a bit without really baking the red earth all around hot enough to fry eggs on. Don Javier sent another work detail out to bury the dead banditos, while Captain Gringo and Gaston took a couple of other peones who knew the area out on patrol.

They found some horse apples southwest of the compound, but the rain had washed away other sign. Gaston observed, "The ones on this side of the house left no brass behind. Ergo, they were a mere distraction, armed only with six-guns. The main force was the one you treated so rudely with the Maxim, my noisy child.''

Captain Gringo nodded and, turning to one of the half-breed mestizos, asked how far the nearest shelter for man and beast might lie from here.

The peon said there were as many dripping trees as one might wish to bed down under, but no nearby settlement. His companion asked what about the Mission San Domingo, and the know-it-all snorted, ''Fool. If they went *there*, the Mosquitos would eat them for supper!''

Captain Gringo remembered something General Portola had said about Dominican missionaries and asked them if the mosquitoes they referred to were mission Indians instead of bugs. They both nodded. One said, ''The Dominican padres doubtless mean well. But in God's truth it is a waste of time for to try and turn a Mosquito into a Cristiano, señores. The padres feed them well and read to them about the wages of sin, but do those naked savages listen? They do not. They are always sneaking off with Don Javier's beef, and when our vaqueros shoot at them for to teach them proper manners, the padres scold us and say we are rude and selfish!''

Captain Gringo had heard that old familiar bitch from ranchers back home in the States. So he cut it short to ask how far the mission was. The peon who seemed to know everything said the Dominican mission was a day's ride, at the head of navigation on the Rio Dorado.

''You can travel on the Dorado by boat?'' Captain Gringo asked hopefully.

The peon shrugged and said, ''By canoe, if one does not mind portage around the many rapids, señor. The padres of course do not have to lift the canoes and supplies they order up the Dorado from the main channel to the south. So they built their mission as far from the San Juan as they saw fit. We, of course, use the trail east to the coast. Cows look most silly riding in canoes, no?''

Captain Gringo chuckled. Gaston asked suspiciously, ''How

is it we find that English couple this far north if they had to pass a mission to get here?''

The peon shook his head and said, ''They would have missed it by three or four kilometers, riding the north–south Indian trail. Don Javier already asked them the same question. The Anglos have no knowlege of this valley, and had they not stumbled into Rancho Trujillo by sheer accident, they never would have made it anywhere.''

His companion nodded and said, ''Even if those ladrónes had not caught them on foot, they would have starved to death. They brought no food with them. They must have thought León was just over the horizon, no?''

Captain Gringo headed them all back to the ranch. It was up for grabs whether they'd been chased by those thugs on orders from the mysteriously mad engineer, Chumford, or just gotten lucky with roving guerrillas. Since whoever the bastards had been were gone, it didn't seem important.

By the time they got back, Captain Gringo's clothes were dry, thanks to the sun. Thanks to the rain he'd been splashing about in earlier, he felt reasonably clean as well as dry. Anyhow, he doubted if they'd be expected to change to dinner jackets that evening.

They weren't. Don Javier and his family lived comfortably but rough and ready. Whatever they were ready for, it wasn't dinner. They kept the snacks and dry sherry coming, and from time to time a peon wandered in to toss another log on the fire. But as the world outside turned deep purple, it was becoming obvious that the Trujillos followed the old Spanish custom of dining late. Captain Gringo nursed his drinks. He knew they could be sitting down to serious eating as late as nine or ten. The fruit, nuts, and tostada dips señora Trujillo and her daughters kept shoving his way had taken the edge off his hunger, and, in truth, if he hadn't been too polite, he'd have been asleep by now. He'd spent more than one long day on the trail and the unaccustomed life of ease was knocking him out. He could see that Ed Palmer wasn't used to the protracted ceremony leading up to a Spanish dinner, either.

The Englishman was drinking too much too fast. He apparently didn't know that when you emptied a wineglass in these parts, someone was sure to refill it. If you even tried to rest half a glass anywhere, Señora Trujillo or one of her daughters was sure to lope over with that damn jug and top it to the brim.

Nature had played tricks on the women of the household. Señora Trujillo had obviously been a beauty in her day. She still had a pretty face despite the double chin. But she'd gotten fat and dumpy presiding over all these before-dinner snacks over the years. Her two daughters still had trim figures. Very nice trim figures, as a matter of fact. But they took after their father when it came to handing out the faces, and while Don Javier was a nice old guy, he was way too homely to consider kissing. Captain Gringo knew he was drinking too much when he caught himself speculating on what it would be like if he could somehow graft the mother's pretty face onto one of her daughter's nice little bodies. He hung on to his glass to keep them out of it as he inhaled some tostada and bean dip to dilute his libido. To get his mind off the subject of impossible if not dangerous sexual adventure, he tried getting more about the mysterious dam project out of Palmer.

The Englishman was even drunker than he looked, it seemed, as soon as he tried to carry on a sensible conversation. But, ignoring the slurs, blank owlish stares, and obvious lack of interest, Captain Gringo was able to establish that the coffer dam, a temporary fill of earth and timbers meant to hold the waters back long enough for the main dam to be built, was already in place and already backing up the Dorado farther downstream. Palmer said the coffer dam would back up a fifty-foot head of water before it crested. Captain Gringo whistled softly as he considered what a flood that added up to, even without the main, higher dam in place to finish off the valley.

He told Palmer what the locals had told him about navigation on the Dorado and asked what sort of vessels the projected locks of the mysterious dam could handle. Palmer took a gulp of wine, shrugged, and said, "If it floats, it'll fit through those perishing great locks. I told them how stupid the design was. I mean, dash it all, no river steamer I've ever seen was more than fifty feet across at the beam, eh what? Chumford's blueprints call for locks a hundred feet across. I ask you, what in blue blazes would anyone do with a bloody ocean liner on a bloody little river like the Dorado?"

"Hmm, if they flood the whole valley, it won't be a bloody little river. It'll be more like a big lake. The contours on my map make it a lake say ten or more miles across and sixty or seventy long."

"So what? Bloody lake won't *connect* with anything you'd want to steam a bloody gunboat or ocean liner up to, what? *I* looked at the bloody map too. The high-water mark will offer them a totally deserted shoreline. The few ranches, villages, and so forth in the valley will all be under water, eh what?"

Captain Gringo nodded and said, "You're right. It's stupid." He caught Don Javier's eye across the room and called out, "Are there any settlements at all on the slopes above this valley, Don Javier?"

The ranchero shook his head and replied, "Not that I know of, and I should know, señor. My naughty cows wander all over the slopes during the wet season. When it is dry, thank God, they know enough to stay down here where the water is all year."

Captain Gringo had neglected to guard his glass during the three-way exchange. So one of the daughters ran over to refill it, giving him a good view down the front of her low-cut blouse. He smiled up at her pleasantly and she dimpled coyly. But, God, what a disgusting sight *that* was. Nice tits just didn't go with old Don Javier's face. It might have helped if she'd had her father's bushy mustache as well as his long nose.

He found her rear view more inspiring as she moved away to fill Gaston's glass. Gaston and Ruth Palmer were chatting in French on the next leather-covered sofa. Her husband was on Captain Gringo's far side and hopefully didn't understand much French, even sober. Captain Gringo tried to catch Gaston's eye as he picked up on their conversation. But the dapper little Frenchman didn't want anyone to shoot warning looks at him. He knew what he was doing. The dumb dame had somehow gotten onto the subject of books. That was okay, but she was talking about the forbidden writings of Sir Richard Burton. *The Perfumed Garden* was a privately printed translation from the Arabic that you had to carry home in a plain brown wrapper after they sneaked it out from under the counter for you.

Gaston's angle was that the Englishman, Burton, had really translated *The Perfumed Garden* from the French, after a young and obviously depraved French officer in North Africa had almost been court-martialed for typing up the original translation in French—plain French—without the Latin terms Burton had used to avoid steaming the glasses of his Victorian readers. Captain Gringo shot a quick glance at Ruth Palmer's husband when she said in French, "Oh, so *that's* what they meant when they referred to the tongue of a woman's privacy?"

Palmer wasn't paying attention. He looked, in fact, like he was about to fall on his face. He probably didn't know as much high-school French as Captain Gringo, anyway. Even a drunk should have noticed when his wife asked another man if it was true that Arabs had longer dongs than Englishmen.

Gaston said modestly, "I have never slept with an English*man*, madame. As for the manner in which a Frenchman probes the depths of Arabesque desire . . ."

"Gaston, for God's sake!" Captain Gringo growled in a no-nonsense tone. The English girl turned, stared innocently at him, and said, "We've been talking about the disgusting habits of the Wogs. Have you ever been in the Middle East, Dick?"

"No. I notice you speak pretty good French, ma'am. Ah, does your husband, here?"

"Heavens, poor Edward can barely understand *English*, after a few drinks. Why do you ask?"

"No particular reason. I read the book. So pray continue."

She laughed and said, "Oh, dear, I seem to have an embarrassment of choices if both you naughty boys are interested in, ah, Arabesque!"

He turned away and got to his feet. Gaston had seen her first, and, in truth, she disgusted him with her brazen flirting in front of her poor dim-witted husband. He meant to smoke alone on the veranda. But of course Señora Trujillo followed to ask him what was wrong.

He smiled down at her in the doorway and said, "Nothing is wrong, señora. I just didn't want to disturb you and the other ladies with my foul tobacco."

"I am called Carlota, Deek. I am most used to cigar smoke."

"Not this kind, ah, Carlota. My last claros have sprouted mold from the damp. But I'm not used to dining late and so I thought . . ."

"Oh, forgive us, we forgot you Anglos eat at sunset!" she cut in, adding something about better smokes as she turned away and started clapping her plump hands for the house servants.

So he didn't get to smoke his moldy cigar after all. They sat down to dinner at last. All but Palmer. He tried to rise and follow them all into the next room, but he only made it to his face on the floor. Don Javier said it was *his* fault, and had a couple of servants carry the dead-drunk Englishman to one of the guest rooms.

By the time they were halfway through the huge meal, Captain Gringo envied Palmer. He wasn't really hungry to begin with, and the local idea of a proper dinner for company consisted of course after course of solid food with wine by the pitcherful to wash it down. Captain Gringo left rude amounts of food on his plates as the servants kept changing them. It was still knocking him out. He could see that old Don Javier, at the head of the table, ate lighter when he wasn't entertaining honored guests. The old guy was getting glazed and dopey, too. His wife and daughters weren't. They just kept shoveling and gulping, course after course. The girls would be as fat as their mother by the time they were thirty, but what the hell, *he* wasn't going to hang around that long.

Gaston and Ruth Palmer had their heads together across the table as they toyed with their food, drank more than Captain Gringo, and talked dirty in French. She kept steering the conversation into oral and anal channels. Gaston kept assuring her that anything between a man and woman that didn't hurt was probably nature's plan. Gaston was welcome to her, orally, anally, or hanging from the roof beams like a sex-mad bat. Captain Gringo wondered idly if Gaston was going to score at all. Dames who talked about sex at dinner parties often seemed to want to say nighty-night with a handshake and a dumb remark about such an enjoyable evening. But Gaston had been around, and if he felt like wasting his time on a prick-tease, who cared?

By the last course, even their hosts were looking whipped. Captain Gringo knew that no polite Hispanic host would ever suggest an end to the entertainment, so he said something about it having been a long day, and old Don Javier looked like a condemned man who'd just been pardoned by the governor as he begged them all to forgive his thoughtlessness and asked his wife to put everyone away for the night.

One of the daughters led Captain Gringo to a guest room, down a long hallway and around a corner into a wing of the sprawling old house. As she placed a candlestick on the oak dresser near the four-poster, she turned her homely face up to him, said, "I am called Susana," and put her arms around his neck to haul him down for an open-mouthed kiss.

She was the one with the longest nose and nicest tits. They tended to cancel each other out as she squirmed against him. Her body felt great in his arms. But her nose felt silly as hell no matter how they tried it. When they came up for air, he warned, "The door is open behind you, Susana."

She said, "I know. I chose this guest room because nobody ever comes down this way at night. My parents and older sister are sleeping in the other wing. Your French friend and the English couple have rooms around the corner."

"Close to each other?"

Susana laughed and said, "Not too close. You noticed what the wife was up to with your friend, too, eh?"

He smiled and said, "They might have known some French words are close to Spanish. Uh, this is a swell room, Susana, but it's late and I'm sort of tired and . . ."

"Bueno," she said, turning away to shut and lock the door, without leaving. Then, as he saw she was slipping her dress off over her head, and how great she looked in the buff from behind, he sighed and gave up on his intended virtue. She was going to be even more upset if he turned her down now. And if her parents found out that she'd as much as closed the door to be in here alone with a stranger, they were bound to assume the worst. So what the hell.

She turned with a shy smile on her ugly face, a vision of voluptuous charm, from the lantern-jaw down, as she walked back bold and naked. He snuffed out the candle as they met for a rematch by the bed.

Kissing her wasn't half-bad, in the dark. Once he learned to ignore that nose, lips were lips, and the rest of her felt fantastic as he ran his hands over her while she undressed him.

He started to drop across the bed with her when he kicked off his dropped pants and boots. But she had other ideas. As she started kissing her way down his naked belly, he realized she'd been listening with interest to some of Gaston's translations of *The Perfumed Garden*. The only thing that kept her from swallowing his erection to the roots was the way her nose rubbed Eskimo kisses in his pubic hair. He laughed aloud as he couldn't help picturing what they'd look like with the light on. He thanked God nobody seemed likely to peek. Hispanics tended to get excited when one merely *screwed* their daughters.

He told her he didn't want to waste it and pulled her up beside him to mount her more sedately. Her body was really beautiful. So when he buried his face in her long black hair to nibble her ear as he humped her, he could almost convince himself she was pretty all over. She responded eagerly and came ahead of him. Then, as he was almost there himself, she suddenly shoved him off and said, "That's enough. I have to get back to the room I share with my horrid sister before she suspects something."

"Swell, but, Jesus, Susana, I haven't *come* yet!"

He reached for her in the dark. It didn't work. She slipped off the mattress, giggling, and groping for her dress on the floor as she said, "You men are all alike. You always ask for more after a woman gives you all you really deserve!"

Then she ducked outside as he rose to go after her. The door slammed in his face, leaving him on his bare feet, bare ass, with a raging full erection, to mutter, "Shit! I don't *believe* this!"

Then he laughed at himself and moved back to the bed. He sat down, shaking his head in wonder. Then he saw a slit of candlelight under the door just slammed on his hard-on and grinned. We were playing games, it would seem. He waited, and the door opened again.

But it wasn't Susana back for a rematch. It was her mother, Señora Trujillo, or, since she was wearing a kimono she'd neglected to fasten securely, perhaps "Carlota" was more suited to the occasion.

The kimono was gaping because the fat woman had the candlestick in one hand and a box of cigars in the other. She saw that he was naked. She saw what he was trying to conceal with his naked thighs as he sat on the edge of the bed. She fluttered her lashes and said, "Oh, forgive me. I should have knocked, but, as you see . . ."

"Yeah, your hands are full. Forgive me for not rising."

She laughed, her plump face flushing, as she murmured, "I see you already have. May I speak frankly with you, Deek?"

"May as well. Your husband's going to shoot us both if he catches us like this anyway."

She closed the door behind her with her more than ample rump and moved to place the cigars and candlestick on the bedside table as she said, "My poor Javier is old and tired. Very old and very tired. I brought you some of his cigars, since I knew you were out of tobacco. But that is not the real reason I came.''

''Well, sit down and let's come, then.''

''Don't be fresh. I am not a wicked woman. I am a mother with a motherly concern for her children. I want you to promise me that when I leave you will lock the door and not let anyone else in.''

''Oh? Who are we talking about, Carlota?''

''One of my girls. Never mind which one. In God's truth, one of them is as proper a young lady as a mother could wish. The other, alas, must be watched.''

He nodded soberly and said, ''Well, you can see she's not here. Would you like to look under the bed?''

Carlota laughed and said, ''Had my wayward child been here, you would not be in the, ah, condition I find you in. Are you, ah, uncomfortable?''

''Very. Would it be asking too much of a gracious hostess if we, ah, did something to ease the pain?''

She shook her head but sat down beside him and opened her kimono more as she sighed and said, ''I am not sure the duties of hospitality go so far, Deek. But, on the other hand, if my wayward daughter were to find you in such an aroused condition . . . well, all men are the same when a woman tempts them, no?''

''Yeah, I'd have a hell of a time resisting temptation right now. But look, as long as you're here to comfort me . . .''

She moaned in pleasure as he took her in his arms and kissed her. There was one hell of an armful. But her face was beautiful in the soft candlelight, and as he lowered her to the mattress and ran his hands over her under the silken folds of the kimono, the sheer novelty of her ample curves began to drive him wild. As he rolled aboard her, she protested, ''Oh, I'm not sure we ought to go so far. Perhaps if I just played with it for you, as a friend . . . I mean, I'm not a wicked woman and . . . Oh, yes, that feels so, ah, proper, after all!''

He fired almost at once, his teased erection ejaculating almost before he could get it in. She felt it, and when she felt that he was still moving after such a quick come, she wrapped her arms around him, hugged him close to her big soft breasts, and crooned, "You certainly know how to flatter your hostess, Deek! We should not be doing this, of course, but since you insist, mi casa es su casa and . . ."

He kissed her to shut her up as they mutually went crazy for a time. She wanted the candle out when he undressed her all the way. That was the trouble with dames who had really unusual sexual scenery to offer a guy. But when he gave it to her dog-style, later, there was enough soft moonlight through the window slits to impress the size of her wide pale rear forever in pleasant memory.

He wanted to share one of her husband's smokes with her and do it some more. But she said he'd already been free enough with her dopey old man's creature comforts, and he didn't try to stop her when she left.

He left the door unlocked after her. At the rate this weird night was going, the other sister or old Ruth Palmer ought to be showing up any minute now.

But nothing like that happened, in the end. In the morning he remembered putting the cigar out somewhere and lying flat with a semisated and still adventurous erection. But there were nights when a guy just couldn't win 'em all, he supposed.

By noon the peones loaned by Don Trujillo had helped the two soldiers of fortune pack their remaining vital supplies four miles or more to the tea-colored Rio Dorado. Others had run ahead to cut and lash together a raft of balsa logs before they got there. So all Captain Gringo had to do was to say adiós and push off down the Dorado.

This far upstream the river was maybe fifty yards across and less than a yard deep between the many sandbars. They had of course lashed the tarp-covered supplies to the middle of the six-by-thirty-foot raft and could manage it pretty well by poling as they stood fore and aft with the cargo between them. Of course, they had their side arms and rifles slung across their backs. The machine gun amidships was primed but under the top tarp, to keep out of trouble and to keep anyone who spotted them from the jungle-lined banks from writing home about it.

As the locals had warned, the Dorado ran south over shallow steps of black basalt placed every few miles. None of the rapids were really dangerous. There wasn't enough current for white-water running. They just had to haul the fucking raft over the fucking black rocks in shin-deep water.

Gaston said he found it très fatigue. Captain Gringo told him it was his own fault, adding, "Never give a dame a lecture on oriental love techniques if you have anything important to do the next day."

Gaston laughed and said, "Merde alors, it was not the modest efforts of that English girl I found such a drain on my strength. I sent her back to bed with her drunken husband after merely showing her how a few positions she said would not work, really worked. I swear I tried to behave myself. But then that damn sex-starved daughter crept into my room after Ruth Palmer left and . . ."

"Jesus, you made it with old Susana, too?"

"Susana? Mais non, she said to call her Alicia. She said she'd had to wait, with her poor dear clit engorged, until her proper little sister went to sleep and then . . ."

Captain Gringo laughed wildly and said, "Never mind. We can talk dirty after we get this fucking raft under way again."

They didn't. They poled around a bend and stopped, letting the current carry them slowly and thoughtfully toward an unexpected cluster of black stone buildings. Some ragged-ass Indian kids were staring at them from the shore. Then Captain Gringo spotted two whiter-looking men in white robes, and when one of them waved, he waved back and told Gaston, "This looks like the Dominican mission we were told about."

It was. The missionaries were friendly and curious. They

insisted on the two adventurers having something to eat and drink with them, even though it was early.

The sun was getting high and hot by then, but the thick stone walls of the mission refectory still held the coolness of night as they sat at the table with the padres, monks, or whatever. The Dominican missionaries were old, gentle-spoken, and obviously out of touch with the world. They'd heard about the dam downstream from worried Indians. They hadn't gotten around to serious worry about it yet. One said, "Here we are in the good graces of the government as well as God, my sons. Neither would allow the strangers from across the sea to flood us out. We have a *mission* here."

Captain Gringo nodded and said he could see that, adding, "The people in charge of building the dam know there are people living all up and down this valley. They know the dam will present a danger to the people living down the San Juan on the far side if it should ever burst. They don't seem to *care!*"

"Then they are evil men, or perhaps only insane, my son. Do you intend to tell them they must not finish their strange structure?"

"Sort of. You're right about it being strange. Can you think of any reason anyone might want to move a steamboat up the river, ah, padre?"

He must have been a priest. He shrugged and said, "There are not enough people dwelling in this watershed to make a steamboat line pay. There used to be quite a bit of mahogany. But most of that has long since been cut and floated down to the boat landings along the wider San Juan, no?"

"If you say so, padre. The river is named for gold. Is there any gold along the Dorado?"

The old man pursed his lips and said, "Sí, a little. From time to time los Indios pan a little in the shallows far upstream. In conquest times, there was some excitement about this. Prospectors searched for the mother lode in the hills to the north. They never found it. They panned such rich placers as there were in the river shallows. All of this, you must understand, was long ago. Now there cannot be enough gold in the entire riverbed to make it worthwhile for a white man to pan. Los Indios have more time, and more modest needs. Even they do not bother much with the fabled gold dust of the Rio Dorado's sandy bed, these days."

Captain Gringo and Gaston exchanged glances. They both said, "Power dredging!" at the same time.

The old men entertaining them just looked bewildered. So Captain Gringo said, "They are installing locks in the dam downstream. Big locks. Too wide for anyone with just a river steamer to need. But in other parts of the world, like the panned-out streams of California, big barges covered with machinery can still show a tidy profit, dredging deep and moving more placer sand in a few minutes than a team of Chinese coolies could pan by hand in a month!"

Gaston nodded and said, "Eh bien, it works, to a point. If the locals can still show any color at all, working long hours with primitive methods, there must be enough left in the way of deep placer to make machine dredging profitable indeed. It's possible some sneaky prospector may have even found the mother lode, higher on the slopes than the pioneers searched. But, as I said, it only works to a point. Palmer says the dam will never hold, once the valley is completely flooded."

Captain Gringo shook his head and said, "It still works, if we assume C.C., Limited, is run by dedicated bastards, and all the evidence so far would show that to be an educated guess."

"Oui, oui, I know about the dam foundations being insecure and all that. But would even a dedicated bastard want to ride a gold dredge down a flash flood?"

"No, of course not. But don't you get it? C.C., Limited, is a *construction* company, not a mining company!"

Gaston gasped and said, "Mon Dieu, that is dedicated bastardry indeed! This species of engineer called Chumford doesn't care how long the dam holds, once he is paid for building it! It's no wonder he sent those hired guns after the

Palmers. He doesn't care what anyone says to the Nicaraguan government, whomever that may be at the moment. He doesn't want the mining interests he and C.C., Limited, are suckering to hear about their très short-term investment, hein?''

They'd switched to English, so Captain Gringo didn't have to watch his language in front of the nice old guys when he said, ''They're a bunch of cocksuckers, too. They might not know they're buying a leaky dam, but by now they must have figured they'll be drowning a whole watershed to muck for low-grade gold. Gold does shitty things to some guys' brains. If someone had told 'em the river sand was full of *tin*, the razzle-dazzle wouldn't have worked.''

Gaston said, ''True. But not even a swinish gold grubber would wish to pay for a navigational system that could wash them all out to sea at any moment. If we got word to them about the unethical methods of their contractors . . .''

''It wouldn't stop them,'' Captain Gringo cut in, explaining, ''Palmer said the dam and locks figure to hold a few months or maybe even a few years. A steam dredge can scoop a lot of placer in even a few weeks.''

''Oui, but when the dam goes, what happens to the gentlemen manning said dredges, Dick?''

''They die, along with everybody else the bursting dam manages to kill. Do you really think the board of directors in London gives a fuck?''

''Ah, true, one hires mere peasants to do the dirty danger-ous work. And of course the company will have had the foresight to take out insurance with Lloyds of London or some other trusting souls. Perhaps a discreet cable to Lloyds of London is in order?''

Captain Gringo shot him a disgusted look and said, ''If you'd been paying any attention at all to Palmer instead of his wife, you'd know it's too late to stop the project any polite way. Even if we could get some big shot in London to listen to a couple of knockaround guys with rewards posted on them, Palmer says the coffer dam's already in place and the water's already backing up.''

"Eh bien, but if they can't get insurance or further funding . . .''

"They go away. Swell. We don't get paid by Portola, because that's not the way he told us to do it. The valley doesn't get saved, either. Abandoned or not, that coffer dam just keeps backing the Dorado until there's a lake at least fifty feet deep behind it. Then, next week, next month, you name it, the temporary coffer dam gives and . . . kablooey!''

Gaston grimaced and said, "You paint a droll, damp picture indeed. Eh bien, I see the only way to get you to shut up about your triple-titted dam will be to help you dispose of it. But have you considered there are only the two of us and a few sticks of dynamite now?''

Captain Gringo nodded, turned back to the old priest, who'd been trying to follow them, with a polite puzzled smile, and said, "Forgive the English, padre. It's better you and your people don't know everything my friend and me might be up to.''

Their elderly host smiled softly and said meekly, "I understand your concern for our political well-being, my son. Unlike our more wordly Jesuit brothers, we have always tried to avoid upsetting our somewhat anticlerical local governments by seeming not to concern ourselves in local politics. Our mission here is only to the poor Indians. In God's Truth, that is enough to keep our order more than busy. Los Mosquitoes tend to backslide most alarmingly when things are not going well.''

Another old man across the table fingered his rosary as he chimed in softly, "Mosquitoes at best give nominal lip service to the true faith when one can keep them well fed and free of serious illness. Let the corn crop fail or the infant mortality rise a bit and, alas, they turn at once to their old tribal spirits for guidance.''

Captain Gringo nodded sagely, as if what they were telling

him was fresh news. He wondered if there was any point to this conversation.

There was. The old priest hesitated, then, in perfect English, said, "You boys are never going to take out those Anglo engineers and their army of hired thugs alone. Give us a few hours and we can round you up at least a platoon of really rotten apples!"

The thirty-seven Mosquito volunteers didn't look like rotten apples. Maybe sprouting mushrooms. It was raining again by the time the Dominicans had called them all in from the surrounding jungle. So each man wore a poncho and low-crowned straw sombrero of mushroom tan. At this late date, most Indian hunters knew how to handle a shotgun. But they'd gotten the message that this was to be a sneaky mission, so they'd brought along hardwood longbows, taller than they were, and packed quivers of reed arrows that rose above their shoulders and almost trailed on the ground behind them. From the little one could see of their shaded faces, they were all grown men. They didn't look savage. They looked like the meek and mild mission Indians they were supposed to be and probably were, when they weren't pissed off.

A few of them had noticed the way the river was backing up down the valley and scouted near the dam site to see why. They'd been shot at. So they were pissed off indeed, and delighted to have a chance to do something about it, with the apparent approval of the missionaries and the more open help of the two soldiers of fortune.

For political reasons, nobody connected with the mission introduced anyone formally to anyone else. The Indians just wandered in from the countryside and lined up along the riverbank with their backs to the mission until Captain Gringo and Gaston moved out to join them. The tall American introduced himself and his shorter sidekick, told them he intended to do something about the threat to their valley, and asked who was in charge and if anyone had any suggestions.

A Mosquito who looked bright and about forty stepped out of line and said he was called Ignacio. He said he was straw boss unless somebody wanted to dispute the matter with machetes. Nobody did. They'd apparently settled a few matters among themselves already, but Ignacio liked to set the record straight. He pointed with his chin at the balsa raft the two adventurers had poled this far down the Dorado and added, "If you wish to carry your supplies closer to the dam site, señores, it will be safer if we pack it by land for you. Those strangers trying for to flood us out have lookouts atop Pocopoco. They have two steam launches cruising the wide waters of the already growing lake upstream. Each launch is armed with a gun that goes cluck-cluck-cluck like a chicken. If they caught us aboard rafts on open water . . ."

"My Mosquito brother's words are wise," Captain Gringo cut in, but added, "How long will it take us, doing it the hard way?"

Ignacio said, "The rest of this day and most of the night, if we only stop for to eat now and then and do not sleep like sissies."

"If it keeps on raining there will be no moonlight in the jungle after dark. Does my Mosquito brother see in the dark like a cat?"

"No, señor. He sees like an Indio who was hunting the slopes of this valley since before most men here were born. I know the best way to flank the dam site. Of course, I am only an ignorant Indio and no doubt they have warned you I am not a good Cristiano, so . . ."

Captain Gringo laughed and said, "You will take the point, viejo mio. You speak of flanking like an old soldado. How many hitches did you do in one army or another, Ignacio?"

"Por favor, it is not wise for a deserter to discuss his military career, Captain Gringo."

"You know who I am?"

"Would we be following you had not the padres told us

there was an outside chance of pulling it off? These muchachos are the cream of our fighting men. The rest, alas, have been wearing pants and praying too long to call Mosquitoes. The strangers down the valley have us outnumbered ten to one. They are in position and primed for an attack. But you are you and I am me. So let's go *kill* the cabrónes!''

Captain Gringo nodded but said, "First things first, Ignacio. I want an organized combat patrol, not a mob. Could you select at least three good squad leaders and figure out who should be holding a strung bow or packing supplies when and if we stumble into anybody important?''

Ignacio smiled broadly and saluted like the old soldier he was before he pivoted on one bare heel and bellowed, "Ramon, Arturo, Fernando! Front and center! Eduardo y Pablo, you two just made supply sergeants. See about getting that stuff off the raft and properly distributed on the backs of the adventurous youths who tagged along despite my warnings of military life!''

As the three he'd selected as squad leaders lined up, Ignacio introduced them to Captain Gringo and Gaston and made them salute, as well as they could manage. Captain Gringo and Gaston returned the salutes gravely. Ignacio said, "Let us be on our way then, my blanco friends. The others can sort themselves out as they follow. We have a long march ahead of us if you wish for to hit those Anglo bastards at dawn's early light, no?''

Gaston shot Captain Gringo a thoughtful look. The tall American nodded slightly and followed the officious Ignacio without comment. He knew what Gaston was thinking, and he too thought Ignacio was acting a little chesty.

Captain Gringo had dealt with pushy noncoms before. Some had turned out to be good soldiers at heart. Others had been simply natural bullies who couldn't handle authority without suffering sudden swelling of the head. Meanwhile, they had a long way to go, Ignacio knew the way, and, most important, the other Indians hopped when Ignacio hollered "froggie.''

Whatever Ignacio was, he had good legs. Both soldiers of fortune were of course legged up pretty good, and even Gaston had longer legs than the squat Mosquito. But Ignacio set a killing pace right off as he started marching south-southwest, trending away from the riverbank. Captain Gringo resisted an impulse to tell Ignacio to slow down. The Indian knew his own people best. If this was a macho display, Ignacio would slow down as soon as he saw that neither white man keeping pace with him was going to whimper about it.

He didn't. But as they reached the tree line, Captain Gringo looked back and saw the others following in good order. Even the men packing the supplies from the raft seemed as well legged up as Ignacio, and the tall American noted with approval that the just appointed squad leaders were in position, with flank marchers out to both sides of the column, arrows knocked in those long wicked bows.

They followed Ignacio into what looked like a solid wall of spinach. But the point man didn't need his machete. He'd hit a game trail he obviously knew. Once upslope in taller timber, the going was open and easy in any direction between the mossy buttressed pillars of the gloomy overhead canopy. The rain was broken by the leaves and branches above into steady streams that looked like monkey piss and felt about as warm when one couldn't avoid it. Ignacio led them upslope at least a mile, then swung south without comment as he spotted some invisible landmark in the seemingly monotonous cathedrallike gloom. Captain Gringo glanced back again and saw that the flank scouts had fanned well out to ghost through the trees on either side at rifle range. He nodded in silent approval. Maybe the old soldier acted self-important because he *was* important, after all.

The tarp-wrapped machine gun and its ammo were being packed a little farther back than Captain Gringo would have chosen, if he'd given the orders. Gaston noticed too, and as he lit a smoke he commented on it in very casual English. Captain Gringo murmured, "Easy hand on the reins, for now.

We're not going to meet the real enemy this side of sunset. So let's keep our enemies down to reasonable numbers.''

Gaston saw that the swaggering Indian ahead of them was out of easy earshot. So he felt free to say, more insistently, ''You have to establish command, Dick. These men are more like the scum we recruited for the old legion than any troops you've dealt with in the past.''

Captain Gringo snorted in disgust and said, ''You forget how far in the past we're talking about. Since the U.S. Army took my old command away, I've led many a guerrilla down here, old buddy.''

''Oui, and as I keep telling you, you are too soft on them. Give a peon one stripe and he thinks he is a general. Take one suggestion and he thinks he is ten times smarter than you are, as well.''

''Stuff a sock in it, you old worry wart. Right now these guys *do* know more than we do.''

''Eh bien, and how long do you think it will be before our bandy-legged cock of the walk begins to wonder why he even brought us along?''

Captain Gringo didn't answer. Gaston made a habit of crossing bridges so far ahead that sometimes they weren't even there. If the Mosquitoes had been up to attacking the dam site on their own, they'd have done it by now.

On the other hand, El Generale Portola had been worried they might. So, okay, he'd have to keep an eye on Ignacio.

It wasn't easy. The runty Indian's legs pumped like steam pistons, mile after mile. The rain let up again before Ignacio did, and it started to get hot, even in the shade, by late afternoon. The soldiers of fortune were dripping enough sweat to stay as wet as ever when Gaston moved closer and asked, ''When are you going to call a trail break, Dick? If I am about to drop, carrying only my side arms and adorable ass, the porters to our rear must really be suffering, non?''

Captain Gringo said, ''If they are, they're pissed at Ignacio, not us. Can't you see the game he's playing? He's sweating like a pig too. He's waiting for me to holler uncle.''

"Eh bien, don't you *like* your uncle, Dick?''

"Hang in there. He can't last much longer.''

"Merde alors, neither can I!''

But Gaston always bitched before he was really hurting, and so he was still moving when Ignacio wavered before a fallen log across his invisible trail, started to step over it, then turned and sat on it instead with an indulgent smile, calling out, "We shall stop here for to piss and rest the weaklings.''

As Captain Gringo and Gaston moved closer, the Indian grinned up at them and asked, "Are you tired, señores?''

Captain Gringo deliberately remained standing long enough to fish out a smoke and light up as he shrugged and said, "I suppose we ought to let the men packing supplies rest now and then.''

"I agree. Give me a smoke, hombre.''

Captain Gringo stared down thoughtfully as Ignacio tried to hold his bold smile. The tall American said very quietly, "Would you like to rephrase that request, soldado?''

Ignacio's eyes dropped first as he murmured, "I was only joking, Captain Gringo. Can't you take a little joke?''

"No. I treat my followers with respect. I expect them to treat me with respect. So don't call me hombre and I won't call you dead. Do we understand each other, soldado?''

"I thought I was at least a sergeant, Captain Gringo.''

"Act like a sergeant instead of a fresh recruit and I'll call you a sergeant. Where were you planning on stopping to cook supper?''

"There is an outcropping of old lava ahead, my captain. We should be there by sunset. There are lava tubes where a man can build a fire without it being seen for miles, eh?''

"That makes sense. Are we within line of sight from those lookouts on Mount Pocopoco yet?''

"Sí, although of course they can't see us under the forest canopy. We are west and thus across the artificial lake from the volcano. I assume you wish for to approach the site by way of El Escudo?''

They were still playing one-upmanship. But Captain Gringo didn't bite. He knew from his tattered map that a lower shield-shaped hill rose west of the dam site, facing Pocopoco across the channel. The map didn't call it El Escudo or anything else. But how many shield domes could there be in the area? He nodded and said, ''Bueno. You must have read my mind. Shall we be moving on, or are you still tired?''

The Indians cooked more than the beans and rice they'd brought along when they stopped for grub in the lava-tube shelter they reached after, not before, sunset. To give him his due, Ignacio led them to the broken-up old lava flow in total dripping darkness, and obviously nobody atop Pocopoco was about to spot a distant cook fire in a cave of glassy black rock.

Captain Gringo rested his back against the rock with his mess kit in his lap as he watched the nearest Mosquitoes torture frogs. The little tree frogs they'd gathered along the way all afternoon were red as ladybugs and covered with the same black dots. For some reason, the Indians had shoved sharpened twigs up the tree-frogs' asses and seemed to be toasting them like marshmallows, alive, over the fire.

Neither soldier of fortune commented. The way a guy learned about native customs was to keep his mouth shut and his eyes open. The Indians didn't seem to be getting any sadistic pleasure out of mistreating the pathetic squirming amphibians, so Captain Gringo assumed they had some reason. The odd colored frogs didn't look at all appetizing as they shone red and wet with sweat over the flickering embers.

The Indian nearest Captain Gringo took some reed arrows from his long snakeskin quiver, and, as the American watched with sudden interest, began to rub the tortured red frog over the darning-needle head of his arrows. Captain Gringo nodded in understanding. He'd noticed that the arrowheads weren't barbed and he'd heard about the poisonous frogs of the rain forest. The cruel display had destroyed his appetite. He lit a smoke to settle his stomach and asked the Indian youth how quickly his poisoned arrows would kill.

The Mosquito smiled modestly and said, "Fresh, like this, within seconds, Captain Gringo. The dry poison we already had on our arrows takes perhaps a minute or so. The padres say it is wicked to treat our fellow creatures so, but if one does not make a frog think he is dying, he does not sweat his best poison, eh?"

"That one's sure sweating. How far off can you hit a man-sized target, every time?"

"To be sure? As far as from here to that mahogany tree down the slope, if one is as good a marksman as myself. I have hit targets much farther off, of course. But if we are discussing men with guns . . ."

"We are. Let's see, that tree outside the cave is maybe twenty yards and, yeah, a barefoot boy with cheeks of tan ought to be able to get that close to a white hired gun." He turned to Gaston, on his far side, and asked, "Are you listening, Gaston?"

"With considerable disgust. I am not too concerned with taking out roving pickets or even outposts. That part would be soup of the duck even for myself and my little knife. But no arrow, poisoned or otherwise, is going to worry anyone inside a *wall!* The other night as I was enjoying the company of that engineer's wife—a man my age must rest between times, after all—she told me something of the layout of the construction site. One gathers she found it très uncouth. But she did say they've cleared the jungle away at least a mile in every direction. The engineers and their workmen dwell in prefabricated frame buildings floated up the San Juan. They are of course on the slopes above the dry channel they've coffer dammed. They are also, of course, well sandbagged and, at night, illuminated by floodlighting. She said that aside from the usual small arms one associates with such activities in primitive surroundings, they have machine guns and, if I

understood her, at least a battery of four-inch howitzers. Little
Ruth was more interested in *my* artillery than any she remembered seeing before she and her husband scampered off. So
she could be wrong. They could be three-inchers, or, merde,
six-inchers!''

Captain Gringo frowned and said, "*Now* you tell me.
Okay, we knew they were expecting trouble. Did she say if
they had their heavy weapons dug in east or west of the dry
riverbed?''

"She was much more interested in Arabesque sexual customs. As a matter of fact, she showed me a trick with her
derriere that was new to me, and I was once stationed in
North Africa.''

"Tell me about it later. This is *serious*, Gaston.''

He took out the map and spread it on the gritty black sand
between them as the Indians went on toasting frogs. He
pointed to the pencil lines he'd made after talking to the
engineer, Palmer, and said, "Okay, here are the two hills, El
Escudo on our side, Pocopoco, the volcano, on the other. The
Englishman said, and these Indians agree, that the coffer dam
of driven piling and earth fill runs so, like a horseshoe, north
of this saddle between the peaks. The lake backed up so far
would wipe out everything below it, all the way to the San
Juan at least, but the flash flood we could manage with the
lake only partly filled wouldn't kill too many innocents
farther downstream. See how the contour lines show the
valley spreading out like a trumpet mouth downstream?''

"Who cares? We don't have enough dynamite to take that
coffer dam out, damm it! The structure is at least fifty feet
thick, and made of soggy timber and loose fill. Even if we
could plant charges against it, with the guards on top able to
discomfort us with well-aimed spit . . .''

"Knock it off,'' Captain Gringo cut in, adding, "I know
how much H.E. we've packed this far. That prick, Portola,
never issued us enough to blow up anything as serious as that
big coffer dam. But we do have a few dozen sticks of

dynamite and our guys have arrows. What would happen if you tied a stick of dynamite to an arrow?"

"You'd doubtless wind up with a faceless Indian or more. Assuming such a droll projectile worked, then what?"

"A stick of sixty-percent Nobel going off against almost anyone or anything out to do some damage and unsettle nerves in the neighborhood. Let that go for now. Got to pick our targets before we aim at them with anything. Did Ruth Palmer even let you in on which side of the dam site the big shots are using as headquarters?"

"Mais non. She was more interested in letting me in other places. I can see by your scribbles you paid more attention to the husband than I did to the wife, conversationally, at any rate. But she seemed so eager to try every chapter of *The Perfumed Garden* and . . ."

Captain Gringo shut him up, put the map away, and called across the fire to Ignacio, "I have two questions, viejo mio. How deep is that water standing above the coffer dam?"

"About twice as deep as you are tall, Captain Gringo. The lake is much broader than it is deep. But the coffer dam will back up a bigger lake at least thirty meters deep by the end of this rainy season. What was your second question, Captain Gringo?"

"What the fuck are we sitting here for? We've eaten supper and tortured all the frogs we caught. Let's move it out. I want to get there before dawn."

Ignacio rose stiffly but said, "I am not certain this is possible, Captain Gringo. We still have a long march ahead of us."

"Let's not argue whether it's possible or not, Sergeant. We have to do it. So let's just do it!"

They did it. Just. A couple of men had dropped out in the jungle behind them and none of the survivors would feel like dancing in the near future, but as the rain clouds began to lighten to the east, Captain Gringo hauled himself up the last few yards atop El Escudo for a look-see.

The first thing he noticed was a white man sprawled nearby, face down in a rock crevice with a reed arrow in his back. Captain Gringo nodded approvingly at the young Mosquito who'd scouted ahead and now sat on his haunches, longbow across his lap with another arrow knocked in place. The Indian murmured, "There is another one, down the far slope. It took longer for the poison to stop his heart. But he did not make any noise and he did not get far."

"Bueno, muchacho. Are you sure these were the only lookouts posted here?"

The Indian looked hurt and said, "If there had been any more, I would have killed them. I moved up here for to scout, as you told me. I was alone here for a moment. Then I heard them coming from down below. I think they must only watch from up here when it is light enough for to see, no?"

"If you're right, that's even better. They'd just been posted. So nobody ought to come to relieve them for at least an hour or so. Move back and get my comrade, the Frenchman, por favor."

As soon as he was alone, Captain Gringo stood up. The guy face down a few yards away was wearing the same nondescript tropic linens and hat. From any distance, nobody was likely to notice he'd maybe grown a few inches.

The tall American stared soberly out and down across the dam site. The map hadn't shown how really big and complicated it was. The rainy dawn was outlining the more imposing mass of the volcano across the way. Smoke rose in thin wisps from the higher peak over there. Either the other lookouts were brewing coffee or Pocopoco was making faces again. It didn't seem to be causing any concern down below.

The floodlights Ruth Palmer had mentioned were winking out as the daylight improved. The result was an even more chaotic view of the big muddy construction site. To the north, the big timber and earth-fill coffer dam loomed higher and more solid than he'd hoped. He saw white-clad figures moving out along its curved crest. On the silvery sheet of artificial lake behind it to the north, a little white steam launch was putting out to patrol already. Had the sons of bitches been tipped off?

Gaston joined him as he was concentrating on the closer site below. The Frenchman remained silent, for a change, as they both stared soberly down at what looked, at first, like antlike confusion. Then Captain Gringo saw patterns emerge. The main housing for both bosses and workers, damm it, clung to the far slope, well up the flanks of Pocopoco. They'd been more worried about rising water than erupting volcanoes, which made sense, when you thought about it. Consolidated Construction, Ltd., was banking on the whole landscape more or less behaving as it had been, recently until they could gut and git. In truth, the nervous Palmer had probably overreacted to the day-to-day tremors of volcanic country. As the light improved he saw there were bushes and even small trees growing both on Pocopoco and this lower shield formation that wasn't supposed to erupt at all.

Thoughtfully, he kicked a loose chunk of old frozen lava and asked Gaston, "Wouldn't you say this hill was a baby brother of the one across the way?"

"Merde alors, who cares? I am not interested in geology. Look at all those *men* down there!"

Captain Gringo followed his gaze. Despite the still-falling rain, the site had indeed come to life now. Most of the activity seemed concentrated in and around what looked like a broad curved roadway running across the dry riverbed between the solid rock walls on either side. He saw that they had the red earth down to bedrock in a lot of places. Lines of workers in peon costume seemed to be trimming the edges of the arched excavation for the main dam. The really heavy digging was being handled by a couple of massive steam shovels. As he watched, the nearest big black excavation machine picked up a monstrous black rock in its reptilian steel jaws and deposited it downstream out of the way. Captain Gringo said, "They sure have a lot of money invested down there. Shame about the workmen, though. I don't like the idea of killing a mess of innocent peones."

Gaston snorted in disgust and growled, "Listen to the child, God. He speaks of sparing lives when anyone can see the only lives in peril at this moment are our *own!*"

He pointed down the hill they were on and added, "Regard what I just spotted between those scrub cedars, my eternal optimist. If that is not an artillery position, what in the devil is it, hein?"

Captain Gringo studied the position below and said, "When you're right you're right. That's a four-inch mountain gun, sure as shit. They're set up to lob goody-goody-bang-bang at anyone coming up or down the valley. There's probably another one at the same elevation on the slopes across the way. The Palmers said they have machine guns as well, and that blonde in Greytown said they were hiring all the gun thugs up and down the Mosquito Coast. But what the hell, they don't know we just took out this lookout position. If they notice us at all up here, they'll think we're the regular guards, right?"

Gaston said, "*This* regular guard is getting regularly wetter and more nervous by the moment. It's almost broad daylight. What are we waiting for?"

Captain Gringo turned, nodded in approval as he saw that the Indians on the back slope were keeping down out of sight as ordered, and told Gaston, "Yeah, we'd better get the show on the road."

He walked back to consult with Ignacio and the others as Gaston tagged along, bitching, "What show? What road? The bastards have cleared all the cover for miles up and down the valley. We are even farther than I thought from the San Juan and the border. But if we duck back into the trees and head south, before anyone comes to relieve those dead lookouts . . ."

"Gaston, shut up. Ignacio, have you explained to your boys how those arrows fitted with dynamite heads are supposed to work?"

"Sí, Captain Gringo. But I don't know myself."

"I've done all the complicated work. The sticks lashed to the arrows are capped and fused. Each archer moves in smoking a cigar. When he picks his target, he lights the fuse and lets his arrow fly, muy pronto. There won't be time to choose another target once the fuse is lit. I cut them short on purpose."

He told a bright-looking Indian to flatten on the rocks topside and make sure they weren't disturbed for a few minutes. Then he took out the tattered map, hunkered down, and called his chosen leaders closer for a council of war as he spread the map out on the rocks.

He gave each squad leader simple instructions they'd be able to remember and told them to get their people out and run like hell the minute things stopped working as planned.

He told Ignacio to pick four good men and stay with Gaston. The Indians didn't argue, but Gaston sighed and asked, "Just where in the devil am I supposed to *lead* this très formidable force, my Napoleonic wonder?"

"You're an old artilleryman. Don't you want to capture that four-incher and see what fun you can have with it? There's only a four-man crew down the slope and they won't be expecting the lookouts posted above them to jump them, so give me time to get into position, and, hell, play it by ear."

"Eh bien, I look forward to training my new gun crew on the job with at least one other four-incher across the way firing counterbattery! May I ask where *you* intend to be while all this très dramatique shit of the bull is going on?"

"Oh, sure. I'm taking the Maxim and a few belts down the slope with me to attack closer in."

On the far side of the big construction site, Wellington Chumford, Esq., stood on the veranda of his hillside quarters, master of all he surveyed as he lit a perfecto. He was a big pudgy man with a florid baby face. Few noticed the cold ruthlessness of his pale blue eyes until it was most unfortunately too late. He was dressed this morning in pale blue silk

pajamas. He didn't have to don his official engineer's boots
and whipcord riding pants unless he had to go down there to
chew out some fuck-up. As he watched his workmen toiling
in the mud and rain, he saw no reason to get wet himself.
Everything was going according to plan. They were right on
schedule. The board of directors had cabled that the local
political opposition was dying down, thanks to the usual
bribery and diversionary tactics of the company's field agents.

One such field agent, the well-stacked blonde Captain
Gringo had met in Greytown a while back, came out to join
him in her own open kimono of strawberry pink. She said,
"Dear, I just felt the house shake under our beddy-bye again.
Are you sure about that volcano looming above us?"

Chumford laughed and said, "It's not due to go off for
another ten years or more. What you felt was blasting. I tried
to tell that idiot, Palmer, that the jolts he was so upset about
were excavation blastings and not his perishing volcanic
tremors. But you know how some people feel about every
little bump in earthquake country." He slipped his free arm
around her silk-clad waist and added, "Speaking of little
bumps, shall we enjoy a quickie before breakfast, my dear?"

Before she could answer, all hell broke loose in the valley
below. The Mosquito archers opened up with their dynamite-
tipped arrows, as per instructions, to clear the area of innocent workmen at the same time they rattled more serious
enemies. The single sticks going off at random all across the
site didn't do anyone they landed near any good, but in truth
most just resulted in considerable dust and noise, lots of
noise, echoing between the opposing slopes as men dropped
picks and shovels and ran in all directions like screaming
ants.

The timing had been carefully planned in advance, of
course. So, before the first dynamite arrow went off down
below, Gaston and his crew had overrun the hillside gun
emplacement and pitched the bodies over the sandbagged rim.
Gaston was already cranking the traverse and elevation wheels
of the little mountain gun as he cursed Ignacio and the other

bemused Mosquitoes in a mixture of Spanish, French, and, thanks to Ruth Palmer's reading, uncouth Arabic he'd almost forgotten. He cursed them partly to keep in practice but mostly for moving so slowly as they passed the ammunition. From here, farther down the slopes of El Escudo, Gaston had a better view of the lower slopes of Pocopoco across the way. He aimed for the place he'd have installed a howitzer over there, if anyone had asked him to, and pulled the lanyard.

Ignacio and the other Indians howled in agony and covered their ears, too late, as the small but big-bored gun went off. Gaston's first shell was still in flight, lobbed high as it would have to be aimed at that range, when he turned and yelled, "Where in the hell is my ammunition, you one-balled camel-fucking bedouins?"

He grabbed a shell from the nearest man, shoved it into the breech, and waited until his first round exploded just in front of his chosen target.

Said chosen target fired a four-incher of its own about then! Gaston yelled, "Hit the dirt!" but remained on his own feet as he adjusted the elevation and fired again.

His second round was on target. Rag dolls, or what looked like rag dolls, flew skyward as the other mountain gun bounced end-over-end down the slopes of Pocopoco. Gaston laughed like a mean little kid and said, "*Now,* my adorable pupils, Papa Gaston will show you how one shoots the liver and lights out of that no-longer-protected housing complex across the valley. But first, dear children, please fetch your dear papa his ammunition. *Move,* you butter-fingered boy-hugging corpse-molesting shit lickers descended from a double-donged ghoul and an ugly but otherwise undistinguished whore!"

As Gaston began to shell the far slope, Captain Gringo broke cover down below, wading out of the brush at the base of El Escudo with the Maxim braced on his hip and the ammo belt trailing behind him like the tail of an enraged dragon.

He fired the machine gun in staccato bursts, saving his ammo for important targets as he made for the nearest steam shovel. A guard who'd flattened in the red dust when a dynamite-tipped arrow landed near him was getting up, levering his Winchester wildly. The next time he hit the dirt with his shot-off face, it looked even more crimson. Another armed white man pegged a rifle shot at Captain Gringo over the crest of a sand pile. There was a panicstricken peon in the way, but tough shit. Captain Gringo blew them both away in one savage burst as he kept moving crablike toward the big black machine. The air around him was hazy with red dust and nitro fumes. So nobody at any distance noticed him in particular in the general confusion. The nearby guards who did were at a distinct disadvantage, as long as his machine-gun ammo lasted. A dynamite-tipped arrow went off close enough to stagger the tall American. Ears ringing, he growled, "Not *me!* You silly sons of bitches!" and hosed the opening in the side of the big steam shovel with the tag end of his first belt before he charged in, tossed the empty Maxim aboard, and hauled himself up into the metal cab.

He'd just determined that any crewmen ever aboard had abandoned ship out the far side, and was on his side, rearming the Maxim with one of the belts he'd wrapped around his chest ahead of time, when some overenthusiastic Mosquito bounced another explosive arrow against the fortunately thick metal roof of the cab. The whole steam rig rang like a monstrous bell, and Captain Gringo bounced off the steel deck, grunting with pain as he found out what it felt like to be the softer-than-usual clapper of said bell!

He rose and seated himself behind the control levers with the loaded machine gun across his lap. He could see out the openings in front and to either side. Behind him rose the oil-fired steam boiler and, hopefully, reasonably bulletproof rear walls of mild steel. The steam gauge said he had a full head of steam. He tried not to think about what would happen if a hard-nosed round punctured the boiler while he sat this close to it.

He'd been at the controls of locomotives, steam tractors, and so forth in his time. So getting the big rig into forward motion was no problem. Neither Captain Gringo nor the designers of the Victorian excavator had ever seen Caterpillar tracks, of course. The steam shovel moved and was steered like a steam roller or farm tractor in reverse. Two huge cleated wheels rose as high as the turntable of the cab on either side up front. They were powered but didn't turn on the chassis. A smaller pair of wheels trailing behind steered the rig like the rudder of a ship.

As he climbed the steep grade out of the main excavation, he experimented with other levers and found that in addition to steering the chassis straight, he could swivel the cab from side to side. The long steel beams of the shovel arm moved in unison with the cab. He'd worry about the way one controlled the inverted-elbow and steel-jawed scoop out ahead of them when he needed to. The fucking rig was threatening to fall over backward as the big front wheels clawed up the steep red clay bank. Then he was over the lip and dragging the chassis over amid considerable dust and scraping. Captain Gringo said, "That's more like it!" as he steered due north toward the coffer dam. Something flew in one side opening and out the other, humming like an angry hornet.

Captain Gringo cursed, threw the levers, and held the machine-gun across his lap to fire as the cab spun merry-go-round on its turntable while the main chassis plodded on to the north. He spotted the two men pumping rifle fire at him from kneeling positions in the dust and let them have a burst as the side opening traversed them. Then he reversed the spin and gave them another burst for luck as he again lined up the cab with the coffer dam ahead.

Someone he hadn't spotted in the dust clouds spanged a round off the blank steel wall behind him. He let it go. He saw, out the right opening, that Gaston was doing a real job on the slopes over that way. A building of some kind exploded skyward in a cloud of shattered lumber and shredded tin roofing. Two tumbling little dots, a pink one and a pale blue one, were about the right size for human figures. But who the hell would be wearing such wild colors?

As the coffer dam's wall of driven piles loomed closer, he saw some white-clad figures above him, firing down his way from the flat crest. He grunted the machine gun around to brace it over the sill of the front opening, and as he opened up with one hand manning the Maxim and the other on the lever that swung the cab from side to side, the results were spectacular. He laughed and said, "Hey, this is neat! If a guy could go into *combat* with a rig like this, maybe a little less clumsy, infantry and even cavalry would be in a hell of a mess!"

He couldn't see the top of the coffer dam from this angle. But if any of the guards he'd put down were still alive, they didn't seem to want to show their heads anymore, so what the hell.

He started playing with the controls of the shovel arm. The movements were jerky and harder to control than one might think, just watching a steam shovel at work. But, okay, this gadget moved the whole arm up and down while this one bent the inverted elbow. When you had the scoop full, the handle up there that looked like a streetcar conductor's bell probably opened the jaws of the scoop and let the shit fall. Hell with it. Wouldn't need it.

The wet timber wall of the coffer dam was impressive as hell, this close to the base. He could see spurts of water making it through here and there the loose fill behind the timber piles. He stopped the rig, squinted thoughtfully, and said, "Yeah, that's the water level on the far side, and we're way *under* it, steam shovel!"

He steered west, moving along the base of the coffer dam in red mud that would have spun the drive wheels had they not been cleated like a farm tractor's. As they protested the ever steepening grade, he told them, "We want to bust this mother where the water level's below the rim of this cab's wheels. They built her like a horseshoe. So if we bust one leg of the arch, the water swirling in sideways and downgrade ought to do some excavating for us as well, see?"

He spied a stream of water shooting out from between two

piles ahead with the force of a garden hose. As he steered even with it, the water washed into the cab across his boots. He said, "This must be the place," and braked the chassis to a halt. Then he swung the cab and boom around to crash the big steel bucket against the soggy timbers of the dam.

Nothing happened to the coffer dam. It made Captain Gringo's ears ring like hell. He grimaced and said, "Okay, let's drop the bucket in the mud at the base and see if we can pull some teeth!"

That didn't work either. He lowered the bucket as far as it would go, then lifted, pressing against the piling. The teeth of the bucket tore long slivers from the damp timber. But he wasn't about to stay here long enough to *whittle* away the coffer dam.

He experimented with the controls, figured out how to hit the mud with the bucket at the right angle, and scooped a wagonload of red muck from the base of the piling. The resultant hole filled with brick-red water by the time he'd figured out how to dump the load and gone back for more. He muttered sarcastically, "Whee, this is more fun than playing in a sand pile," as he got the hang of it and started digging a serious hole.

Then a woodpecker started tapping on the metal all around him, hard. He dropped to his knees behind the controls, sighting along the barrel of his own Maxim for the source of the other machine gun fire. A blue haze hung above the coffer dam on the far curve of the horseshoe. He shrugged and said, "That's long range for automatic fire, friend. But, okay, if you want to play."

He fired his Maxim back in short bursts, more to keep the other machine gunner pinned down than with any hope of hitting the son of a bitch. The prick was firing down and across from a break in the ragged top ends of the coffer-dam piling. The guy was good. Captain Gringo saw, after he'd lobbed a few bursts into the cordite haze across the way, that his worthy opponent was ducking between his own bursts. Captain Gringo would have liked to do the same. But he couldn't excavate dry river bottom, man his own Maxim, and watch out for flanking rifle fire all at the same time with his head below the steel sill of the cab!

He moved the boom to his right, so the big bucket and its heavy steel arm was between him and the enemy machine gunner. It meant starting a new hole and prevented him from returning the bastard's fire, but as bullets bounced off the bucket instead of his forehead, he decided it could have been worse. He kept one eye on the rim of the dam above as he chewed up red mud at its base. He saw he'd accidentally done a good deed by digging a little farther from the base when the hole started to fill fast with what looked like boiling tomato soup. At the same time he spotted dots moving along the rim above and said, "Oh, you wanna get *closer?* Be my guest, motherfucker!"

There was a natural loophole formed by two piles having been driven deeper than the others. He knew the gun crew moving to flank him would spot it too. So he shifted the Maxim, sighted on the skylight filling the gap, and, the moment someone filled it with his head, fired a long hot burst.

As is often the case in combat, Captain Gringo couldn't say for sure whether he'd blown someone's brains out or just made them duck. Nobody was firing at him with anything from any direction now, so he assumed he'd at least made the other old pro reconsider his options.

As he scooped up another wagonload of river bottom, Captain Gringo began to reconsider his *own* options. The water-filled excavation was overflowing and running downslope toward the old main channel of the dammed Dorado. More red water gushed skyward from the center of the pool as if a water main had burst somewhere down there. More water, this stuff whiter, was streaming from the timber piles to his left. He nodded and said, "Right, she's undermined and ready to let go, so what the fuck is a nice boy like me doing in a *river bottom* like this?"

He scooped up the Maxim and jumped from the cab with it

cradled in his arms. He hit the red mud and it came up and over the tops of his mosquito boots. He growled, ''Oh, no, not *that* shit again!'' and started floundering up slope, the mud trying to suck his boots off with every step. He was maybe fifty feet toward higher ground when he saw his shadow outlined by bright orange across the red mud. Then the shock wave hit him and threw him face down in the mud on top of the Maxim!

The earth still trembled like jelly and the whole valley reverberated echoes of the tremendous blast when Captain Gringo pulled his muddy face out of the red goo, cursing and spitting red slime. He looked back over his shoulder, saw the huge mushroom cloud of red dust and blue smoke, and grinned. Naturally any construction site included an explosives dump, and Gaston, bless him, had hit it!

Then he saw what was happening closer, just beyond the steam shovel, and struggled to his feet. It wasn't easy. He was plastered with what felt like pounds of mud, and it kept sucking at his boots. But he had to get moving pronto, so he did. He left the Maxim wherever it was in the mud. He'd used up almost all the ammunition in any case, and if he hadn't, he still needed high ground more than he needed anything else.

He almost made it. He was actually clear of the mud and was running fast up the drier slope of the Dorado's flood plain when the Dorado burst through the coffer dam and went crazy for a while.

The lake backed up behind the coffer dam tried to get through the first modest gap all at once. As Captain Gringo had foreseen, the raging waters tore across the valley at a forty-five-degree angle, washing far up the slopes of Pocopoco to swish the debris of the smashed-up construction camp back into the old channel in a rainbow arc of swirling, roaring, and oddly screaming chaos. Some of the screams were no doubt human.

Then the whole undermined coffer dam gave way and things got even wilder. Captain Gringo had made it well

above the former banks of the Dorado, but the river didn't
pay attention to former banks or even the laws of gravity. A
four-foot wall of foaming water caught up with the tall
American and knocked him flat. Then, as the surge ebbed, it
tried to suck him back down the slope into the swirling
confusion of timber-studded whirlpools and cross-currents.
He grabbed something solid and hung on as the water poured
the other way over him for a million years. Then he could
breathe again and saw he'd been clinging to a well-rooted
scrub cedar that would never be the same again until it grew
lots of new branches. He said, "Thanks, bush," and got to
his feet to run uphill some more before the river sloshed back
across the valley.

He rolled over a basalt outcropping, tore through more
scrub, and stopped on a rise to get his bearings. He was up on
the slopes of El Escudo. He spotted cordite smoke to the
south and headed that way, calling out to Gaston and his gun
crew, if that was them making all that noise.

As it turned out, Gaston was alone in the sandbagged
emplacement. He pulled the lanyard, turned as the four-
incher lobbed another shell across the valley, and, spotting
Captain Gringo, said, "Ah, there you are. Pass me some
ammo, will you? My stupid Indians seem to have run away
for some reason."

Captain Gringo asked, "What in the hell are you shelling?
Is there anything *left?*"

Gaston turned to peer over the sandbags, shrugged, and
said, "Eh bien. Perhaps they've had enough for now. I still
see little white dots moving up the slopes of Pocopoco
though."

"Big deal. There were some survivors. Hopefully most of
the innocent workers made it before the dam went. That was
the idea of the dynamite arrows. You say Ignacio and the
others ran away?"

"Oui; I fear he did not have the vocation for soldiering he
boasted of. I think it was that explosives dump going off that
unsettled them. I don't remember seeing anyone around me

here when I picked myself off the bottom of this adorable dusty pit. Do we really have to go looking for them?''

"No, they know the way home, and, thanks to you and me, they'll still have a home to go to for a while. How far do you figure we are from the border?''

"We could make it just as the border patrols are taking la siesta, if we hurried, Dick.''

"Okay, what are we waiting for? Let's hurry!''

The bank had just closed for the weekend when the two soldiers of fortune made it back to San José, Costa Rica, a few days later. Gaston of course would have bitched all weekend about not being able to cash the rubber-wrapped check he'd carried all this way, if Captain Gringo hadn't shut him up. The tall American said, "Give me the damn thing and I may be able to work something out with a lady I know at the cable office. It won't kill us if I can't. Thanks to our getting back here the hard way, we still have the pocket money we left Greytown with.''

Gaston said, "True. But the only trouble with Costa Rica is that there is no market for our skills in such a quiet country. We're going to have to make ourselves more presentable before we can check into even a modest hotel and...''

"Give me the damn check," Captain Gringo cut in, adding, "Barber shop is down this way. We'll get shaves and a haircut, get rid of these rags, and still have enough to live on for a month.''

"Perhaps, but not *well*, my Spartan youth. I was looking forward to at least two, ah, skilled masseuses willing to join me in the steambath I must have to restore my poor old joints, after all those primitive nights on the trail, hein?''

Captain Gringo laughed and said, "Now I know I'd better cash that check. I don't want you blowing my half, no matter how good they blow at that steambath of yours!''

Gaston handed it over as they went down the arcade to the

barber shop. They got cleaned up for pennies in American terms, and the simple linens they replaced their trail-worn duds with cost little more than denims would have back in the States. As they lit new Havana claros out front, Gaston counted his change, shrugged, and said, "Well, maybe one masseuse will be enough. The usual hotel, later?"

"Right. It's better to check in separately. Some of those latest reward posters mention us running in pairs. Meet me in the bar around nine, or, if either of us get lucky, I'll see you for lunch mañana."

They split up, Gaston heading for his notorious steambath, as they called it, and Captain Gringo heading for the cable office.

Costa Rica was one of the few places he didn't have to worry about meeting cops staked out in public places. He was looking forward to a long visit, if this check didn't bounce. The only fly in the ointment of San José was that the local government here was too easygoing and stable for a knockaround guy to make a living with a gun.

The cable-office lady executive he knew, in the biblical sense, wasn't in. She'd taken off for the weekend, too, damm it. Captain Gringo didn't try to cash the foreign check with any of the snippy-looking dudes on duty there that afternoon.

As he turned to leave, he noticed a nice-looking redhead, dressed like an American Gibson Girl who planned on playing tennis in the near future. She had to be a gringa. It wasn't his problem. At least, it wasn't his problem until she followed him out of the cable office and called his name.

He stopped, turned, and ticked the brim of his new planter's hat as she smiled up at him. He asked, "Do I know you, ma'am?"

She said, "Call me Vera, Dick. It's silly to make up fictitious last names, don't you agree?"

"Yeah. Your accent gives you away as a Brit. I sure hope you're not from British intelligence, Vera."

"Lloyds of London. An underwriter for Lloyds, and I'd rather not go into it, I've been expecting you to show up here.

You see, we know about the cashier's check that poor Portola gave you."

"I hope when you call El Generale poor you don't mean he hasn't got the money to *cover* said check, doll!"

"He's dead. Some maniac named Morales assassinated him the other day for reasons the powers that be are still working on. The general's bodyguard blew the assassin away before anyone could question him. If you try to cash that mysterious check the general gave you, who knows who might want to question *you*, Dick?"

He frowned down at her and asked, "Why is Lloyds of London so worried about my health, Vera? I don't remember taking out a policy with *any* insurance company lately!"

She laughed, locked her arm in his, and said, "You'd play hell getting anyone to insure your life at the moment. But we do want to pay you off. Come with me. I'm staying near here. I have your agreed-on price and the promised bonus as well, in cash, waiting for you there."

He didn't argue. He let her lead him meek as a lamb to slaughter as she went on explaining. She said, "We're an insurance company, not a charitable organization, so naturally we want some small favors from you and Gaston Verrier."

"Naturally. Who does Lloyds of London want bumped off?"

She laughed and said, "You two already did quite a job on the scamps who were trying to take advantage of us, Dick. The first thing you do when I give you the money will be to tear up that check, agreed?"

"That sounds reasonable. I wouldn't have been able to paste this check in my scrapbook as a keepsake no matter *who* cashed it. Get to the second line of the fine print, doll."

She led him around a corner and into a narrower side street as she told him, "By Monday the international press should be carrying full details of the terrible volcanic eruption, earthquake, and flood you lived through, poor baby. The first reports were confusing and conflicting, but this morning a British engineer named Palmer cabled from Greytown, reporting the way everyone had ignored his warnings about Mount Pocopoco.''

Captain Gringo laughed and said, ''Palmer was nowhere near the site when we took it out, and he was wrong about the volcano. Pocopoco never blew. I expected it to, after the shaking we gave the whole area, but . . .''

''You're not *listening*, dear,'' she cut in, adding, ''C.C., Limited, took out a heavy policy insuring them against failure to complete that dam. They offered a pretty premium. But even so, our underwriters didn't want to go for it at first. After all, building a dam in earthquake country in the middle of a civil war does sound a bit risky, eh what?''

''But you did insure them, in the end.''

It had been a statement, but the redhead took it as a question and explained, ''Not fully. Our underwriters said they could insure the site against acts of war or acts of God, but hardly *both*! The company took the word of their own geologists and settled for *war coverage*. Is a picture emerging from the mists yet, dear?''

He laughed and said, ''If the *London Times* says it was an act of God, who am I to argue? Now that I think back, Gaston and me were nowhere near the place when whatever happened happened.''

She said he was learning, and led him into a patio through an archway. He didn't see anybody pointing a gun at him from the shuttered windows all around, but that reminded him of other questions, so he asked her, ''How come your agents in Greytown tried to stop us from signing on as hired guns for the outfit, if you didn't want them wiped out by an act of war?''

She hesitated, then said, ''My, you *do* play chess, don't you? All right, Dick, since it's over, you may as well know. We didn't want you anywhere near that dam site, no matter which side you started out working for. We were afraid that once you saw that the little people you seem so fond of were going to be flooded out with no compensation by the project, you'd do, ah, just about what you did. But all's well that ends well. So now we can all be friends, eh what?"

She led the way to an oak door set in the far stucco wall of the patio. As she unlocked it, she explained, "Your money's waiting on the bed inside. I didn't want to chance carrying so much cash on me. So..."

And then Captain Gringo stiff-armed her through the doorway, hard, and followed her into the darker shade, fast, whipping out his .38 with the other hand. He dropped to one knee and kicked the door shut behind him with his boot heel before crabbing to one side, ready for whatever came next.

The redhead lay sprawled across the bed in the center of the room, face down and skirts up around her hips as money fluttered down like confetti on and about her bare fanny. There was nobody else in the one rented room.

He got to his feet, putting the .38 away as he said, "Sorry. Once upon a time a lady told me a fib and I've never gotten over it."

Vera rolled over and sat up, leaving her skirts up around her hips. He supposed she might be feeling the effects of the tropics, even though she wore no underwear under that thin white dress. She smiled up at him uneasily and said, "Heavens! Anyone can see it's cheaper to pay a man like you off than it would be to *kill* him!"

"That's true. Even if this had been a setup, and even if it had worked, you kiddies would still have Gaston to deal with, and he showed you in Greytown that he's tougher than he looks, right?"

She nodded eagerly and said, "That's what I just said! You and Gaston Verrier are dangerous to mess with, you just saved my company millions in any case, so I was told to pay you off, get you to agree about the cover story about the washed-out dam on the Dorado and... Why are you looking at me like that, Dick? I'm an insurance adjuster, not a lady gun-slick, and you're frightening me with that cynical smile and knowing eyebrow! I swear I've nothing up my sleeve. I swear what you see is what you get, and, oh dear, how can I convince you I only want to be your friend?''

He reached behind him to lock the door latch as he told her, in a much friendlier tone, ''Oh, I'm sure we'll think of something, once we put our heads together.''

The Best of Adventure
by RAMSEY THORNE

"THE KING OF THE WESTERN NOVEL" IS *MAX BRAND*

5 EXCITING ADVENTURE SERIES MEN OF ACTION BOOKS

___**NINJA MASTER**
by Wade Barker
Committed to avenging injustice, Brett Wallace uses the ancient Japanese art of killing as he stalks the evildoers of the world in his mission.
___**#5 BLACK MAGICIAN** (C30-178, $1.95)
___**#7 SKIN SWINDLE** (C30-227, $1.95)
___**#8 ONLY THE GOOD DIE** (C30-239, $2.25, U.S.A.)
(C30-695, $2.95, Canada)

___**THE HOOK**
by Brad Latham
Gentleman detective, boxing legend, man-about-town, The Hook crossed 1930's America and Europe in pursuit of perpetrators of insurance fraud.
___**#1 THE GILDED CANARY** (C90-882, $1.95)
___**#2 SIGHT UNSEEN** (C90-841, $1.95)
___**#5 CORPSES IN THE CELLAR** (C90-985, $1.95)

___**S-COM**
by Steve White
High adventure with the most effective and notorious band of military mercenaries the world has known—four men and one woman with a perfect track record.
___**#3 THE BATTLE IN BOTSWANA** (C30-134, $1.95)
___**#4 THE FIGHTING IRISH** (C30-141, $1.95)
___**#5 KING OF KINGSTON** (C30-133, $1.95)

___**BEN SLAYTON: T-MAN**
by Buck Sanders
Based on actual experiences, America's most secret law-enforcement agent—the troubleshooter of the Treasury Department—combats the enemies of national security.
___**#1 A CLEAR AND PRESENT DANGER** (C30-020, $1.95)
___**#2 STAR OF EGYPT** (C30-017, $1.95)
___**#3 THE TRAIL OF THE TWISTED CROSS** (C30-131, $1.95)
___**#5 BAYOU BRIGADE** (C30-200, $1.95)

___**BOXER UNIT—OSS**
by Ned Cort
The elite 4-man commando unit of the Office of Strategic Studies whose dare-devil missions during World War II place them in the vanguard of the action.
___**#3 OPERATION COUNTER-SCORCH** (C30-128, $1.95)
___**#4 TARGET NORWAY** (C30-121, $1.95)

DIRTY HARRY
by DANE HARTMAN

Never before published or seen on screen.

He's "Dirty Harry" Callahan—tough, unorthodox, no-nonsense plain-clothesman extraordinaire of the San Francisco Police Department...Inspector #71 assigned to the bruising, thankless homicide detail...A consummate crimebuster nothing can stop—not even the law!

___# 1 DUEL FOR CANNONS	(C90-793, $1.95)
___# 2 DEATH ON THE DOCKS	(C90-792, $1.95)
___# 7 MASSACRE AT RUSSIAN RIVER	(C30-052, $1.95)
___#10 BLOOD OF THE STRANGERS	(C30-053, $1.95)
___#12 DEALER OF DEATH	(C30-054, $1.95)

To order, use the coupon below. If you prefer to use your own stationery, please include complete title as well as book number and price. Allow 4 weeks for delivery.